Me No Pause Me Play

MANOJ KUMAR SHARMA

INDIA • SINGAPORE • MALAYSIA

ISBN 979-8-88521-237-3

Disclaimer: Reader friends and others, please note that this is a work of fiction. The characters, places, businesses, technologies, practices, events, incidents, and everything else mentioned in the book are the products of the author's imagination and have been used in a fictitious manner. Any resemblance to any person, living or dead, place, location, business, incident, event, practice or technology is purely coincidental and the author cannot be held responsible for the same. Reader friends and others are requested to treat the essence of this story as fictional material and nothing more than that.

Dedication

This novel is dedicated to my mother, Late Hem Lata.

This novel is also dedicated to all women.

Special Thanks

To all the Book Lovers, Readers, Reviewers, Critics and Literature Houses who loved my debut novel, MIRRRO, and encouraged me to do more and more storytelling.

Contents

Preface

In today's advanced world, even though a lot has been said and a lot has been done for Gender Equality, Women Liberation and Women Empowerment; patriarchy and misogyny still surface every now and then across the globe.

Seems that the women-empowering doctrines exist only in law, literature, preachings and the virtual world, whereas, practicalities in real life are often quite contradictory.

Though for ages, women have been worshipped like goddesses in *Sanatan Dharma* and a few other civilizations, out of autocratic convenience men always intent on being the boss of women.

The gap between preaching and practising never ever seemed to marginalize and continues to widen beyond tolerance.

This story reflects all odds and evens of society from the micro perspective of women.

Instead of feeling pity for the struggling women amid endless suffering, the story manipulates the best footprints of male DNA to rejuvenate the disintegrated female DNA in an innovative way with calculated risk.

The story not only revives the bettered version of women's life but takes it to the next level by sparking inspiration for the current and coming generations of women.

Let's hope that despite nature's cruel chorus, women can sing "Me No Pause, Me Play".

Acknowledgement

Thanks from the bottom of my heart:

- To my nation 'India'
- To my family

Chapter 1

Paused

31ˢᵗ March 2025, Monday

02:30 PM

31ˢᵗ Floor, Womanica Worlds

Andheri (West)

Mumbai

"Womanica Wooed Women WorldWide!" Rajat Khanna exclaimed proudly after displaying the slide over the screen, in front of the top delegates of the company, ace investors, foreign investors, media, social media influencers, prominent figures from the cine & fashion industry, political fraternity and lucky guests selected from among the customers.

Attendees of the Annual Corporate Meet applauded in rejoice and many of them gave a standing ovation. Rajat was in seventh heaven as he continued addressing the audience. "And it's my immense pleasure to share with all of you that Womanica not only wooed women all over the world but maintained its top position for the third consecutive year. It's a hat-trick, guys. Hat-trick!"

The conference hall once again thundered with claps.

"It may be the opposite as well. Women Worldwide Wooed Womanica," a senior colleague commented loudly in the crowd.

The unnecessary comment annoyed Rajat a little, but his vibrating mobile phone disturbed him. The caller was the society's secretary. *"When will these jokers learn not to call at the wrong time?"* He thought and ignored the call. Then, as if not have heard the comment, he continued, "Friends, can you guess, who actually deserves the credit of our success?"

Quickly glancing at many hands being raised one after another, Rajat galloped in sarcasm with a slant smile. "But, please, no wishy-washy answers. Unique answers only." Pointing at one of the attendees, he said, "Yes, friend. Yes. The man in saffron shirt. Please speak."

"Sir, the best quality of our products," expressed the guy.

Rajat was about to speak, but his mobile started bothering him again. He cancelled the call once again. He continued, "No, no, no. See, all top 10 companies, worldwide, are offering the best quality products. One can't deny it." Looking around, he pointed towards another guy. "Yes, friend in blue shirt. Please."

"Sir, our expertise in sales & marketing," the guy speaks out.

"No, no, no. See, nowadays every company is using aggressive sales and marketing strategies." After a few seconds of pause, he said, "See, guys, please don't look at our success through the lenses of your departments only. The quality guy is claiming the best quality, the sales & marketing guy is claiming the best sales & marketing practices. Grow up, guys. Please widen your vision and rise above the bar. Think beyond your horizons. Anybody else?" Rajat spoke like a business philosopher.

His mobile started irritating him again. He took out his mobile and gave it to the stage manager to talk to the caller.

In the meanwhile, when he saw no hands raised that time, upset Rajat preferred speaking profoundly. "See, gentlemen, if you carefully look into the journey of our consistent success, you will find that it's our company's prudent approach towards women and womanhood, which enables us to deliver the best quality products and in achieving absolute customer satisfaction. It's our loving, respectful and caring mindset towards women, which enables us to win their hearts.

Our competitors create products mechanically, whereas we create products emotionally. Our competitors sell things using modern-day sales & marketing gimmicks, whereas we sell things using age-old human-to-human emotional bonds. Our competitors treat women as a commodity, whereas we value women as our own responsibility. Practically saying, most of our competitors don't care for the real needs of women but try to impose their products on them. Whereas we put women foremost, understanding their desires behind the needs and then delivering accordingly.

It's the DNA of this great company, which transforms people working here by developing a character that intrinsically loves and respects women and does everything to make their life better.

So, guys, from the bottom of my heart, it's a humble request to everybody in Womanica Family to ensure consistent caring, valuing, loving and respecting women, and these positive emotions will keep us driving towards the success of Womanica. Thank you."

Loud claps were followed by standing ovations for such a powerful speech, and the Meet continued.

Immediately after delivering the speech, Rajat stepped down from the dais and moved towards the stage manager waiting for him outside. Without asking anything about the calls, he took his mobile phone and called the secretary. "What the hell has happened? Why you were calling me so impatiently?"

"Mr Khanna, it is my duty to call you in grave situations. But, as usual, you don't have time for anybody," Mrs Gupta said.

"What do you mean? What happened?" Rajat reciprocated.

"Mr Khanna, your wife is admitted to the ICU in City Hospital. It is an emergency. You must come here ASAP. Anything can happen; she is in danger," Mrs Gupta said humbly.

"What? What are you talking about? She was ok in the morning. What happened suddenly?" Rajat shouted.

"Mr Khanna, I can't tell you everything over the phone. The doctor has called me, so I am going inside the ICU. You, please, come here immediately. It's the hospital's policy to take a relative's approval before starting an operation. So, come fast," Mrs Gupta said in a single breath.

"Operation? What for?" Rajat screamed, but the call had already been disconnected.

Suddenly, Rajat felt like falling from the seventh heaven, from a graceful to grim situation. "What the hell could have happened to Dolly that led her to ICU? If there hadn't been the need for an operation, I would have avoided it. But, right now, I will have to be there."

He informed his boss, Mr Shaurya Bansal—MD, Chairman and Promoter of the company—and headed towards City Hospital.

As soon as Rajat reached the ICU, he met Mrs Gupta in the Visitor's Lobby, who was waiting for the doctor's update on the operation. He almost lost his mind when she updated him on what had exactly happened.

As usual, that morning the maid came at 11:00 AM and rang the doorbell. However, she didn't get any response from Dolly, even after trying multiple times. She tried to call her on mobile. The ring was audible outside the door, but Dolly was still not responding. More than half an hour passed, the desperate maid then contacted their immediate neighbour, Mrs Gupta, the society's secretary.

Mrs Gupta also rang the doorbell and called Dolly, but there was no response. Then she called the maintenance guy to hang a rope ladder and find the insights of Dolly's apartment on the 11th floor. She also called a key maker to make duplicate keys to open the door.

After approximately one hour, a maintenance worker succeeded in viewing inside Dolly's house. Mrs Gupta was shocked to hear that Dolly was lying in the washroom, half-naked and bleeding from the head.

Mrs Gupta was trying to connect with Rajat. She called up a few more ladies from the society to get help. Meanwhile, the key maker came, and within an hour, he succeeded in opening the door. Mrs Gupta along with the ladies rushed to the washroom.

Everyone was shocked to see the blood dripping from the head, forming a pool. Two of them immediately did her first aid to stop the bleeding. One checked breathing, which was very low. They tried to talk to her, but there was no response, even after many attempts. They somehow managed to lift her and placed her in bed. Mrs Gupta started giving a massage to Dolly to normalize her condition.

A few minutes passed, but Dolly didn't show any signs of improvement, which bothered Mrs Gupta and the crew. Then suddenly, Dolly coughed in unconsciousness. Mrs Gupta felt that she might need water. When she tried to give her water, she didn't swallow, and it spilt out from her mouth.

Sensing something serious had happened, Mrs Gupta called Rajat, which he never answered. Finally, she decided to call an ambulance and admit Dolly to a hospital.

As soon as Mrs Gupta finished briefing Rajat, the doctor called her. While heading towards the ICU, she didn't forget to remind Rajat that she called up him hundreds of times, and he didn't answer. The wooden-faced Rajat ignored her and followed her to the ICU.

Rajat was disheartened on seeing Dolly lying unconscious in the ICU bed. Several tubes, pipes and wires were attached to her body. Her face was covered with an oxygen mask. She was surrounded by various equipment and monitors. He tried to ask something, but Dr Kaushal, the floor doctor asked them to join him in his cabin.

The doctor showed them Dolly's reports and started updating them about her condition. "Sir, the patient is still unconscious, after approx. 6-7 hours of the incident. The prima facie feedback from Mrs Gupta, and even the initial test reports, suggests that the patient fell and her head hit the floor, which caused a severe head injury and bleeding.

We conducted all the necessary tests—Blood Test, Urine Test, Oxygen Level, X-Ray, Sonography, Citi Scan, MRI—as soon as the patient was admitted. And I have just received all the preliminary reports. These reports indicate:

1. A few blood clots in the brain because of the head injury. It needs to be operated on, if possible. Sometime back, when she regained consciousness, I tried to interact with her and noticed that her memory and speech could be affected.

2. Half paralysis in the right side, mild in nature.

3. Mild convulsion attack; that's why she is put on a ventilator.

4. Blood loss; we are already transfusing blood.

5. The gynaecology reports indicate that she is in the menopause phase.

6. No medical history of blood pressure, diabetes was found in the patient's old medical files that Mrs Gupta brought.

We are closely monitoring her condition. The next 48 hours are highly critical. If she shows signs of significant recovery, then we can plan the next course of treatment.

As far as the blood clots are concerned, we have two options. If we want to resolve the issue immediately, then operation is a must. But, even for the operation, we will have to wait for at least 48 hours to allow her to recover from convulsion and blood loss and get her into a stable condition. Else, we will have to allow it to heal with time. How much time it will take to heal naturally, can't be predicted. Maybe 6 months, 12 months, or 2 years."

"Ok. Then do the operation as soon as her condition permits," nosy Rajat said.

"Sure. But, we need your written approval," Dr Kaushal said.

"Ok. Get me the document. I will sign it right away," Rajat reverted impatiently.

"No. Not right now. It will be required, just before the operation. But, till that time your presence here in ICU will be highly expected because she is still in danger," the doctor said.

"By the way, how much time will the operation take?" Rajat asked.

"It would be a minimum of 5-6 hours." Dr Kaushal reciprocated.

Rajat thanked the doctor and came out of his cabin. He, then, thanked Mrs Gupta for her help and expressed that she could leave, as he would now be present there.

It was already 5 pm. Rajat was very upset about the untimely emergency. He cursed Dolly for falling into this dire situation at such an important moment of his life—when he was on the verge of getting a much-awaited promotion to the highest position in the company as

Managing Director. Considering his consistent dynamic contributions and role in maintaining the company's top position in the market for three consecutive years, the promoter of the company decided to delegate the responsibilities of Managing Director to Rajat, who was currently holding the position of Deputy Managing Director.

At night, while resting in the ICU dormitory, he spoke to his son, Akshay, who was settled in New Jersey, USA as the Vice President of a top brass IT Company. Akshay's wife, Pooja, was a Fashion Designer.

"Hello, Akshay," whispered Rajat.

"Yes, Dad. I am listening."

"Akshay, your mother is very serious. She is in ICU."

"Oh! My mother? She is your wife, too."

"What? How are you talking? Have you gone mad? Is this the way to talk to your father at such a grave moment?"

"Dad! I am talking in the same way you taught us."

"What nonsense are you talking? When did I teach you talking rubbish like this?"

"Since my childhood, I have seen you talking like this only, with Mummy, Anjali and me."

"Why you are raking up the old issues when I am under tremendous pressure," Rajat yelled over the phone.

"Pressure. Tension. You are always under pressure and tension. We have never seen you without pressure or tension. You, yourself, create pressure and tension and then you torture us to get rid of your pressure and tension. Anyways, leave it. You are never gonna improve. Tell me what happened to your wife?"

"Your mother fell in the washroom. She got a severe head injury, blood clots in the brain, half paralysis and a convulsion attack. She is in ICU in a very critical condition. She will have to be operated on for blood clots in the brain. I am feeling very nervous, being alone to handle this situation. I was hoping you and Pooja could come here to look after her," Rajat uttered humbly.

"Now, I understood. You want to run away from your responsibilities towards your wife. You are still more concerned about your job. That's why you are asking us to come down there. I am shocked to hear about my mother. I feel very upset and sad for my mother, but I don't have any sympathy for you. You never ever did anything good for your wife. At least now, in such a situation, you must leave your professional commitments and dedicate your time to your wife."

"Son, forget the past and get ready to handle this life-threatening situation," requested Rajat.

"Son? Surprising!" Akshay said sarcastically.

"What surprise?" Rajat intervened.

"First time in my life, I am hearing this word for me from your mouth. See..." Akshay confronted his father, but Rajat jumped in.

"No, no, no. Don't speak like this."

"See, I can do anything for my mother, but I will not do anything for your wife. And this situation can't compel me to extend any help, even if I wish," Akshay said bluntly.

"Why?" Rajat asked inquisitively.

"Pooja is six months pregnant. So, sorry, even if we wish to come, we can't come." Akshay reasoned his stand and terminated the call.

Now, Rajat understood Akshay's grievances towards him, which led him to confront him, even in such a life-and-death situation. Apart from that, his wife's advanced stage of pregnancy could also have been the reason behind his reluctance to come there.

Immediately after that, Rajat called his daughter who also was in the USA. She was there with her husband in Michigan. Her husband was a banker there, and she was working as a Sanskrit Teacher in a local Government School.

"Hello Anjali," whispered Rajat.

"Yes, Dad! How are you? How is Mom?" Anjali asked surprised because Rajat never called her since she shifted to the USA after her marriage.

"Beta! We are not in a good condition. Your mother is very serious. She is in ICU. Actually, she—" Rajat paused.

"What happened, Dad? What happened?" Anjali almost screamed.

Rajat told Anjali everything in detail and requested her to come there.

Anjali, deeply saddened after hearing the recent update about her mother, without any second thought, said, "Dad! Don't worry. I will be coming there. Let me arrange everything, then I will inform you.

After a few hours, Anjali informed Rajat about the arrangement of the tickets and promised to keep him updated with the Visa status.

That night, Rajat couldn't sleep.

Firstly, he was very much upset with Dolly. What the hell was she doing in the washroom that made her fall, making herself bed-ridden and spoiling the most precious and awaited moment of his life?

Secondly, he was frustrated with his son, who always speaks shit against him. The one whose birth was celebrated in the best possible way with huge hopes of getting support in old age.

On the second day, in the morning hours, Rajat was updated by the doctor. Dolly was still unconscious with fluctuating oxygen levels, temperature, blood pressure, creatinine level and many other parameters. Given that there had been no significant improvement, the operation had to be further delayed.

Three-four days passed. Dolly's condition was the same, rolling over like a roller coaster ride. Anjali's visa was awaited, precisely speaking, taking its official time of 15 days.

Meanwhile, Rajat was in constant touch with his boss and kept him updated about the situation.

Sometimes, he thought of asking somebody else to stay with Dolly like Mrs Gupta, another neighbour or somebody from his office. But, the doctor refused to allow anyone to stay other than a close family member. So, he was eagerly waiting for his daughter to come and handle the situation.

After fifteen days, Dolly's health condition was still in the doldrums. Sometimes, it appeared to be improving significantly, but the next moment it was sinking again.

Rajat was now frustrated. He couldn't attend his office in the last 15 days. Colleagues, friends and neighbours used to visit, consoling him with hopes for the fastest recovery of his wife. He had no relatives in Mumbai, and he didn't bother to inform anyone else. His boss also visited once and advised him to come out of the situation fast, else he may miss the chance of promotion that year. Those discouraging words of his boss were escalating his frustrations with every passing moment.

Out of sheer hatred, he was not picking up calls of Akshay or his wife. But, he was in touch with Anjali as, more than Anjali, he was waiting for her visa.

On the sixteenth day, he received the good news from Anjali that she had gotten the visa for three months. She would be reaching Mumbai the day after and promised to call before the take-off.

The next day, in the afternoon, he got a call from Anjali, who was crying unstoppably and couldn't even speak clearly. "Dad! Dad, I couldn't board the plane."

"What happened? Why?" asked puzzled Rajat.

"The airport authorities are telling me that as per the rules, ladies with advanced pregnancy of 7-9 months are not allowed to travel by air. Since it is the 9th month of my pregnancy, they didn't allow me to check-in."

"Oh my God! Then how did they issue the visa? Didn't the authorities know the rules?"

"I asked them. They said they can't be answerable for others' mistakes."

"But, why didn't you tell me about your pregnancy? Even Dolly never told me."

"What to say, Dad? Everybody in our family knows about it. We talk about it almost every day, chat about it in our WhatsApp group. But you are not in that group. You are never available. How to say, Dad?"

"But, why am I not in that group?" Rajat intervened.

Sobbing, Anjali continued, "Dad! Everybody avoids you because of your rude behaviour, everybody fears to face you, even all of our relatives. Please, Dad, improve yourself. At least, now it's time to control your anguish, and please learn to behave politely. We know how rude you had been with Mummy. Now, it's time to treat her with love and kindness, after all she has been your wife for 30 years. Please, Dad, are you listening to me?" Anjali spilt so many bitter truths in a single breath.

"Hmm... Ok. Then you please go back to home and take rest," reddened Rajat mumbled and cut the call.

Anjali sobbed 14,000 km away. She understood how her father must be feeling after hearing her hurtful words.

The father, who was eagerly waiting for the daughter a few moments ago, was now cursing her for daring to teach her father about the art of behaviour and wasting his time giving him false hopes for the last 17 days.

By this point, Rajat's annoyance was fully blown. His shrewd mind was conspiring how to manage and get rid of this life-spoiling situation.

"Sir, Doctor is calling you." The voice of the nurse disturbed his thoughts.

He followed the nurse towards the ICU.

The doctor was near Dolly's bed, discussing something with a nurse. As soon as Rajat reached there, he started updating him. "Sir, just a few minutes ago she again got a mild convulsion, so we need to put her on the ventilator again. We need your approval."

"Do whatever you need to do. Why do you always need my approval?" Rajat asked in a harsh voice.

"Sir, we need to follow our SOP, that's why," the doctor explained.

Rajat intervened and yelled loudly, "What bloody SOP? What is this drama going on for the last three weeks? Every day you are telling a new story. First, you told me that the blood clots need to be operated on. Then after some days, you said that the operation can't be performed now. What the hell are you people doing? Sometimes you say that whatever happened was because of the symptoms of menopause, and the other times you say that it was because of low immunity level and weakness. Are you experimenting with the patient's body? Or have you opened a shop for milking money from dying people? Are you even a genuine doctor or have you gotten a fake degree? I don't even know if Dolly is alive or dead. Bloody, my life is paused. I am not going to tolerate any more. If you people don't cure her within the next 7 days, then I will sue this hospital in court."

"Sir, sir. Sir, please calm down. Calm down." The doctor tried to pacify Rajat.

"What bloody calm down? You calm down. Now I don't have trust in you. Don't talk to me. I would like to talk to the owner of the hospital. I will talk to the owner only. Tell me, where can I catch him? Tell me, I say," shouted fully frustrated Rajat.

Dolly was sleeping under the influence of the morning dose of medicines. The other patients and visitors started looking at him with fearful curiosity. Two nurses went out to call security to control Rajat.

"Sir, sorry to say, right now the owner is not here. But you can meet our Managing Director, Dr Dave," the doctor requested.

"Ok. Then escort me to the place of Dr Dave." Rajat grunted in controlled aggression.

"Yes sir. This is Sister Nirmala. She will take you to Dr Dave."

Sister Nirmala guided Rajat to Dr Dave's swanky lavish office on the top floor. Rajat was asked to wait and told that he would be called after 5 minutes.

5 minutes, 6 minutes, 7 minutes, 8 minutes passed, but still, Rajat didn't get any call from the Managing Director.

For half an hour, he was trying to restrain his negativities. But now, his annoyance blew off beyond the limits; his face turned red and blue, and his eyes heated up. He stood from his place and headed towards Dr Dave's opaque cabin. The security guard gestured to wait. Rajat turned down his request. He pushed the door, entered the cabin and closed the door from inside. At the very first glance, he saw the rear side of the MD, sitting on the lavish revolving chair.

"Excuse me," Rajat uttered softly controlling his annoyance.

Hearing those words, the chair gently revolved and the angelic eyes of the graceful mesmerising Dr Dave met with the fiery eyes of Rajat.

"You?" exclaimed the MD in sheer astonishment.

"You?" screamed Rajat in an unexpected shock.

Chapter 2

Past

"Oh my God! What the hell! You? Here? How?" the perplexed MD exclaimed.

"Oh! What a coincidence! After such a long time, it's you, Jasmona. That too, like this, here?" said Rajat.

"I joined City Hospital yesterday. Today is my second day," Dr Jasmona Dave responded in quite a formal way, subsiding the emotional excitements.

"Oh, nice. Actually, my wife, Dolly, is in ICU. That's why I am here," Rajat also responded formally now.

"What happened? Is anything serious? Let me check, and," Jasmona had to pause to attend a call.

The call was from the Owner & Chairman of the City Hospital, Dr Ayushi Bharati. While attending the call, her expressions kept on changing wildly, intermittently staring at Rajat with rotten expressions. She finally concluded the call assuring her best. "Don't worry. Let me handle this. I will take it as a personal challenge. Okay. Bye."

   Me No Pause, Me Play

After the call, she closed her eyes for a few seconds with some deep thoughts as if self-talking. After a minute, she asked, "So, what were you telling me about your wife?"

"She is in ICU for the last three weeks, and I am not happy with the way treatments are going on. There is no clarity. Seems like the doctor is following the trial & error method," groaned Rajat with mild annoyance.

"Hmm. Let's check up on Dolly," Jasmona decided and then moved towards ICU.

Jasmona carefully watched Dolly's condition, who was still sleeping.

She had a discussion with the doctor and team and reviewed the daily logs. She asked the team to come to her cabin along with all the reports for an urgent meeting and asked Rajat to wait outside.

After the visit, Jasmona comprehensively reviewed all the reports and the medical history of the patient. She discussed the case with the team and also via a conference call with the visiting expert doctors.

By evening, after a lot of brainstorming, she decided to go ahead with the operation to remove the blood clots. Though the team of ICU doctors and expert doctors, expressed their sheer reservation against the operation, but Jasmona was Jasmona. Her risk-full adamant decision forced them to not prolong the argument and join her for the operation.

She had microscopically studied the brain blood clots' size, pattern and effect over Dolly's body, convulsion patterns and frequency, extent and severity of half paralysis, gynaec status and its effect over the body and other key parameters contributing to Dolly's overall health conditions.

She called Rajat and briefed him about the need for an immediate course of action.

"But, a couple of days ago, the doctor told me that it was too late for an operation. Then how is it possible now?"

"What do you want? You want your wife to get normal at the earliest, isn't it? That's what I am doing. I am overruling the doctor's decision. Do you have any problem with that? The blood clots in the brain are a critical ailment right now, creating various problems for her body. So, first and foremost, I have decided to get rid of those blood clots. By operation, the clots will be removed immediately. It will take much more time if we try medication. I will treat her simultaneously for other problems. Now, is that clear?"

"Ok, do whatever you can do. I still trust you."

"You must trust me. Is there anything else you want to know?"

"When is the operation scheduled?"

"We are working on that. Within a couple of hours maybe. We will let you know. Till that time, please wait in the visitor's lobby."

Rajat was a little happy about the quick actions taken by Jasmona but upset about her rude behaviour. He wanted to be with her or around her, but she bluntly asked him to stay away.

Jasmona was not the kind of person she was being in front of Rajat. The reasons for her rude behaviour were known to both of them.

After skipping lunch, Rajat was feeling very hungry. So, he decided to have a heavy dinner, after which he sat in the dormitory as he was waiting for the call.

While waiting he thought about the turbulent past few days, with a variety of shades: hope (Anjali's planned arrival), despair (Anjali not being allowed to travel), his ignorance towards family (he is not aware of the happenings in his family), family's hatred towards him (nobody in the family likes to talk to him), being preached (Anjali telling him to improve his behaviour), getting a surprise (meeting Jasmona), memories (seeing Jasmona after 30 years, the past life reeled like a film and the memories aroused mixed emotions), emotionlessness (Jasmona's unfriendly behaviour was discomforting him), healing (Jasmona's decision about the operation), job pressure (the frequent calls and threats from the boss).

But, now, Jasmona was there. He believed she would set everything right as quickly as possible. Dolly would regain her health and get well very soon, and he could resume his office. It was a once in a lifetime happening that the chair of the Managing Director was being transferred to an employee. He had immense faith in Jasmona that she would make everything alright.

"Sir, Dr Dave is calling you," the voice of the nurse stilled his thoughts.

"Ok," reverted Rajat and followed her.

"We will conduct the operation tomorrow morning at 10. It will take 5-6 hours. Till that time, please be patient and be present outside the OT. Before the operation, you will have to sign the consent form. Anything else you want to ask?"

"No. Nothing. I will be there."

"Good. One more thing, after the operation, I need to have a talk with you, Dolly, your other family members, the neighbour who admitted Dolly here and the near and dear ones. I need to contact anyone who can help me investigate the root cause of this problem so that I can find out a permanent cure. I need the contact details of all these people. Is that clear?" asked Jasmona without any expressions on her face.

"That's ok, but I can tell you all the details that you would need for your investigations. Even Dolly can help you with your research, once she is conscious. But why do you need to contact the other people."

"Who is the doctor, you or me? Who is treating Dolly?" Annoyed Jasmona shook Rajat with her crisp words.

No words came out of Rajat's mouth. He just stared at her. He couldn't afford to reflect hatred or annoyance in his eyes. For the first time in his life, he felt like prey in a helpless situation.

"What happened? Don't have any answers? I know you very well, Rajat. You need to unlearn your superiority attitude. Please do whatever I ask you to do, and don't do anything to annoy me. Is that clear?" Jasmona shocked him yet again.

Rajat got up from the chair. Without making any eye contact, he turned back and started moving out. Midway, he raised his hand and grunted, "Tomorrow morning I will be there at the right time." Saying that he quickly left her cabin, all the way he wondered what happened to her and why was she behaving like that.

A naughty smile of sarcasm spread over Jasmona's face watching Rajat. "This is nothing Rajat. It's just the beginning. You will have to face a lot more," whispered Jasmona sarcastically.

The next day, while waiting outside the Operation Theatre, for the first time in his life, Rajat felt like the most helpless man in the world. Nothing was in his control. He couldn't even influence anything. On the contrary, he was dependent on the mercy of others. The pity situation was hounding him like hell.

"Congratulations. The operation is successful." Jasmona's sweet voice pulled his attention.

"Thanks, Jasmona. I am really really thankful to you."

"Oh! Come on Rajat. Thank God. Today, He was with us."

"Yes, that's right. But, the way you have taken the risk and made such a difficult decision, you really deserve accolades." Rajat was trying hard to please her.

"That's ok. Now, after the operation, she will be unconscious for a few hours. I will examine her as soon as she is awake. Till then, take some rest. I am going to attend a meeting," Jasmona said formally and left without giving him a look.

Post-operation, Dolly's health was moderately recovering with each passing day.

However, as she was having multiple health issues, it was taking more time for Jasmona to crack the complexity and identify proper strategic treatment for faster and satisfactory recovery from a long-term perspective. That's why she was waiting for Dolly to recover to the extent when she can start proper flawless communication with her. At the same time, Rajat was advised to stay back at the hospital only to attend to the frequent requirements of medicines & consumables and any emergency that could be expected at any point in time.

After approximately two weeks, Jasmona's expectations came true. The efforts of the dedicated team of doctors, nurses, physiotherapists and psychiatrists paid off reasonably well. Dolly had recovered significantly in terms of various physical parameters. She was quite comfortable listening, understanding things and responding to people around her, but she had difficulty in speaking. The picture of psychological aspects was still not so rosy. She couldn't be exposed to any stress, else her condition could deteriorate. She was suffering from depression and anxiety and often feeling low.

However, Jasmona was confident that with diligent precautionary measures while interacting with Dolly, the root causes behind those psychological pitfalls could also be identified and considered for her treatment.

So, one day, after completing her morning visits and meetings, she decided to get involved personally and started talking to Dolly directly.

"Hi, Dolly!" Jasmona greeted her with a Duchenne smile.

"Hi," Dolly whispered in pain.

"I am Dr Jasmona Dave, MD of this hospital. I am handling your case. I have visited you many times, but couldn't speak to you. How are you feeling right now?"

"Lot of pain. Not good," stammered Dolly.

"Oh! But don't worry, as now I will be here with you. Everything will be fine very soon. Now listen," Jasmona was coming to the point, but Dolly intervened.

"How?" Dolly was getting emotional.

Jasmona sensed the depressed emotions. She held Dolly's hands into hers, massaging them softly to soothe her and said in a soft voice, "Don't worry Dolly. All will be well very soon. I am your doctor, but please consider me as your sister, your close friend. Ok?

See, for your faster recovery, apart from the medical treatment, I need to know about some personal things from you, which you might hesitate to share with anybody else. But, by doing this, you will be helping yourself as well as me to treat you better. You got my point?"

"What do you want to know?"

"No, no. Not right now. It's enough for today. Let's talk for some time daily to avoid any stress on your mind and body. Have you noticed, that despite the paralysis, how well you could speak today? That's what I want. I want you to be like you were before, even better than before."

"Yes. Feeling sad being bedridden. I want to go home," Dolly whispered with shuddering lips.

"Yes, definitely. You will come out of this bed very soon. Now, you take some rest. I will come in the evening." Jasmona said quickly and left as she couldn't see Dolly's depressed face.

That evening, after fulfilling all her commitments, Jasmona took Dolly on a wheelchair ride in the garden area. The hospital staff and Rajat were surprised at Jasmona's gesture as the ICU patients were not supposed to roam outside.

After seeing the joyous and positive reactions of Dolly while and after the ride, Jasmona decided to have the chat, not in the hospital building but, in a natural environment. She convinced Dolly for three rounds of rides in the morning, afternoon and late evening and instructed her staff to schedule her courses and medications accordingly.

That day onwards, Jasmona succeeded in gelling emotional bonding and developing a healthy friendship with Dolly. Within a few days, Dolly also found a true friend and trustable ally in Jasmona.

That was the magic touch of Jasmona, but looking from the other angle, she was just doing her job and working very hard to meet the commitments she had made to the management.

Jasmona and Dolly started with their talk sessions. Rajat was always kept away during this routine.

As the discussions continued, a dark picture of Dolly's life was brought to light.

The unfortunate day was the 30th marriage anniversary of Rajat and Dolly. Rajat had a marathon of important functions and meetings in the office the whole day. He wanted to be in a good mood and fully charged so that he could handle all the official activities with a stress-free mind. He wanted to enjoy the day without missing anything. That's why before leaving home, he wanted to celebrate their marriage anniversary by having a couple of rounds of intimacy with his wife.

However, Dolly was not feeling well. She had been feeling painful hot flashes the previous night and spent the whole night with no sleep. Since morning, she had been feeling giddy & nauseous. She spewed a couple of times, leading to dehydration, weakness, low energy and even fainting. She was finding it very difficult to stand in the kitchen to prepare breakfast. She was not comfortable even while lying in bed or sitting on the comfortable reclining sofa.

She had been facing similar symptoms for more than a year. The reason, told by her gynaecologist, was that she was one of the sufferers of the worst symptoms of menopause. Menopause is a natural process that every mensurating woman has to face. However, unconfirmed reports indicate that one in a hundred million cases are observed, where the worst symptoms are quite difficult to handle, leading to death-like situations. Therefore, she needed a comprehensive treatment for dealing with this transformation.

Rajat was least bothered by the medical complications of Dolly's poor health. His sole focus was his job, and at home, he wanted a fully devoted wife, obeying his orders and fulfilling his desires, unconditionally. For him, menopause was a common thing in any woman's life and suspected that Dolly was using it as an excuse to avoid him.

That morning, because of intolerable health conditions, Dolly was finding it very difficult to meet his expectations, which annoyed Rajat. Desperate Rajat then shamelessly attempted the so-called marital rape, but, failed because of her dry passiveness.

Frustrated, Rajat broke the coffee pot by slamming it on the floor. He hurled abuses at Dolly and warned her of dire consequences if she didn't serve him better. He, then, left for his office banging his feet loudly on the floor, murmuring derogatory comments.

Rajat's behaviour broke Dolly into thick tears and endless cries. She couldn't understand how to cope with the situation and deal with her husband. Amid heart-breaking cries, she again felt like throwing up. With tremendous pain, she somehow managed to get up from the bed and limpingly rushed towards the washroom. She spewed, which drained out her leftover energy. Within a few seconds, everything went dark and blank.

When she came back to her senses, she found herself in the hospital surrounded by nurses and doctors. She felt numbness in her body, specifically in the right half. She tried to speak but couldn't. Her eyes closed again and she went into unconsciousness.

Thus, the prospects of grand celebrations of the 30th marriage anniversary were jeopardized, because of insane reasons, but she believed that her abnormal menopause ruined the occasion. The previous day, their children, settled in the USA, spoke to her and asked about the plans for celebrating the anniversary. But, her passive reply didn't surprise their children, because they very well knew what kind of a person their father was.

This single incident could reflect the quality of relations between Rajat and his family members. But, things were not always the same.

Dolly shared how in the initial 3-4 years she had been living in heaven. Those were the golden years of her entire life. Rajat was a happy guy, joyous and always smiling.

In those days, Rajat was very romantic, like filmy heroes. He was a loving husband who was drowned in the sweet sugary love of his wife. He always used to speak things that pleased Dolly and do things that made her happy. He used to admire her beauty. He was a diehard fan of her deep eyes, rosy lips, graceful face, beautiful long hair, figure, style of speaking, way of walking and body language. He used to say that Dolly, his wife, was the most beautiful woman on earth.

She remembered, in those days, he was a fantastic entertainer, too. He used to sing filmy songs, especially romantic songs at her request. Often, he would make her laugh, hysterically, by doing mimicry of various film actors, political leaders, sportsmen and various other characters. He used to organize and participate in parties, family get-togethers and annual Ganpati, Durga Pooja, Deepawali, Holi and New Year celebrations. People around had a lot of appreciation for him.

When she was not in good health, he would ask her to take some rest. He would take leave from work and do all the household chores. She used to feel fortunate to have such a nice human being as her husband.

But, the scenario changed drastically after the births of their children, one-after-another in two consecutive years. Even though they had planned the second baby after a gap of 5 years gap, when she conceived Anjali, they restrained themselves from an abortion.

Initially, they had ample time for each other, but after the birth of their very first child, their son, her priorities changed. Somehow, she managed timings to discharge her duties as a mother and wife. But, a few intermittent gaps in paying attention towards her husband, the beginning of mild rifts among Dolly and Rajat. It seemed that Rajat had still not matured enough to understand Dolly's responsibility towards her child.

When their daughter arrived, Dolly was almost clueless. Whom to look after? Whom to leave? Whom to give priority to and whom to not? The infant daughter, one-year-old son, husband and last but not least, herself. She catered to the intermittent cries of the children throughout the night, whereas Rajat used to wait for her and get inadequate sleep himself.

For two years, life was like a bed of roses and, now, like a bed of thrones ornamented with roses. The fragrance and feel of roses disappeared slowly. While discharging the needful duties towards the children, she couldn't get time for the desiring husband or even herself.

Those natural situations were drawing invisible lines of emotional parting between the husband turned into father and the wife turned into mother. However, Rajat's priorities didn't change. Instead of understanding the situations with a mature mindset, putting in efforts and taking up equal responsibility, Rajat clearly said that he was very busy shaping his career and did not have time to handle kids, but used to expect the same intense dedication and attention from Dolly.

Days, weeks, months and years passed. Dolly spent her life measuring the time through her children. She brought them up with utmost love and care, focusing on their character building, behavioural science, the Sanatan art of life, best health practices, best education, extra-curricular activities, sports, etc. She was the best mother in the world according to Akshay and Anjali, and they requested her many times to participate in the competitions of Best Mother Awards, but she turned down their requests smilingly by saying that what she had done was her duty.

However, the children's opinion was not the same about their father. Since childhood, the duo had seen their father in a serious mood, aggressively talking over the phone or to their mother or themselves about their report cards. Though their report cards were always in good shape, he had complaints. He asked them to improve further and become excellent. He was never happy with the moderate results. They never saw a smile on his face. They never found their father talking to them peacefully or humbly, as fathers of their friends generally talk to their children. They never saw their father talking to their mother on good terms. They never saw their father socialising with people.

Often, in the morning hours, they saw their father yelling loudly over his phone as instructing people for some official issues or on their mother for his morning needs and often blaming her openly for not being attentive. Evening hours they never found the father at home.

But, in late evening hours, when they were amid deep sleep, Rajat's loud phone calls often disturbed their sleep. Not only that but, often in late evening hours, they heard him shouting loudly over their mother for various issues while drinking peg-after-peg and polluting the home ambient with his chain-smoking, and they had to witness and tolerate his such rogue arrogant behaviour throughout the day. He never took them for any outing like for movies, children's parks, shopping malls, gardens, picnics, long drives, etc.

Whenever they asked their mother the reasons behind his rude behaviour, she blamed the extreme job pressures for transforming their once jolly father into a temperamental person. She used to blame the job culture, work environment, survival crisis, unrealistic business targets, etc., which led their father to lose control and delve into drinking and smoking as a way to bust stress.

But the children never got convinced. As per them, in their friend circles, everybody's fathers were known as busy people in their career or business, but they behaved very nicely at home and in professional and social life. Even rare were the cases, where somebody was known as a smoker or drinker.

But, Dolly was always speaking as a wife, with her commitment to protecting her husband's image, irrespective of public opinion around.

Dolly expressed, in a nutshell, that such a nice guy had unfortunately fallen into the trap of consequentialities of life or precisely saying failed to manage the consequentialities of life and mutated demonic shades into his character with each passing day.

To compensate for the absence of regular intimacy with his wife and to subside the stress out of the acute job pressure, he started depending on insane stress busters of drinking and smoking. And the dependency over the stress busters soared with time and became essential habits of his life. More than that, exhibiting behavioural disorders under the influence of intoxications also rose with time. All good traits of his character diminished with time, and in the family and society, he was being known for his various demonic traits.

But, a few fortunate things also happened in his professional life. He changed organization and joined a manufacturing company as Senior Manager – Accounts. There, his hard work was recognized and appreciated from time to time, and he rose the ladders of success very fast. Currently handling the responsibilities as Deputy Managing Director of the company. That company was in the business of manufacturing various products for women, like beauty products, apparel, clothing, dress materials and many more. His hard work brought the company on the threshold of global levels of business.

However, his successful ride in the job, couldn't improve his family life or his relations with his wife and children. On the contrary, he got transformed into a more aggressive person. Dolly wondered, it was the continuously mounting responsibilities and business pressure taking a toll on him. But, she came to know from his few colleagues that not always but sometimes in office and meetings, he was a very nicely behaved and well-mannered gentleman. That meant Rajat was changing his face at his convenience.

Though Dolly was understanding each and every happening in his life and in their lives, she intermittently attempted to help him in dealing with the odds in his life, precisely speaking, in dealing with the odds in their intimate life. However, she didn't succeed because of the absence of suitable timings and his unworded adamancy for satisfying male domination unconditionally.

After a lot of failed attempts, Dolly left everything in the hands of God and in the hands of Time, and she left herself flowing with the natural course of life. She focused on the quality upbringing of their sweet children but, at the same time, kept an eye on Rajat's lusty desires.

Like any ordinary wife-cum-home maker, Dolly was also hopeful that sooner or later, one day, her husband will get changed into his best old avatar. A sweet loving husband, full of joyous and humorous offerings for wife and children. The memories of his entertaining skills, singing, mimicking, joking and many more used to make her hopeful about him. Despite all the odds, Dolly didn't want to lose her husband or even take any legal action by divorcing him or charging him with domestic violence and marital rape.

Time went by. Meanwhile, the children also got married. Surprisingly, Rajat didn't participate actively in the arrangements of the bride for the son and the groom for the daughter. Everything was done by Dolly. Rajat was there in marriage ceremonies, just fulfilling the formalities as a father, irritating everybody present there.

Both son and daughter got settled in the USA.

Then came the oddest period of Dolly's life, when she started experiencing strange symptoms in her body. Though her gynaecologist was taking care of her very well, she warned her stating that her case is not normal.

Dolly's physical and mental health was deteriorating with each passing day. More than a year passed like this, even though the treatments were in place. But now, the egotist Rajat, blinded by his success, couldn't understand what the hell his wife was going through, or he didn't want to understand. Even during the lockdown in the pandemic era, Rajat didn't spare her. The whole lockdown period he spent working from home, boozing, smoking and targeting Dolly for satisfying his desires. Dolly was always shockingly surprised that even at this elderly age, having married children who were expecting their next generations to be born, how could Rajat still have an unquenchable hunger for lust.

Finally, that unfortunate day came because of which Dolly met a wonderful person like Jasmona.

One day, Dolly burst into emotions. "I don't know why, but whenever I used to see you, I forgot my problems, my health issues. Your graceful beautiful face, your speaking and smiling eyes, your sweet voice, your style of talking, your sweet smile, your behaviour. Your personality altogether always brings hope in me that an angel has come in my life, who not only will heal my physical and mental illnesses but also heal my husband and our sore relations.

Jasmona felt deeply emotional after hearing Dolly's story, which furthered her sense of responsibility towards the patient coupled with her commitment to the organization. She thanked God, who protected her from such a husband, else she would also have suffered like Dolly.

Despite being a very professional doctor, Jasmona felt an odd emotional attachment with Dolly. She would boost Dolly's morale. In one of the chatting sessions, Dolly talked a lot about the stress caused by menopause. Jasmona told Dolly to deal with the stress by chanting a catchphrase: **"Me No Pause, Me Play."** It meant, whatever be the situation, whatever goes against me, I will never ever pause or stop me. So, I will play. I can't control or fight nature, but I will continue playing in my life like an innocent child.

Dolly religiously followed Jasmona's valuable advice and chanted, **"Me No Pause, Me Play."**

Many rounds of personal discussions, created a final picture, which caused a lot of turbulence in the analytical mind of Jasmona. What she understood was that there were two epicentres of concern for Dolly.

Firstly, Dolly's menopausal complexities were causing serious effects on her mental and physical health, which led her to the current condition.

Secondly, Rajat's unruly demonic behaviour was responsible for Dolly's mental trauma up to great extent. If Rajat could improve and return to his jolly, joyous, charming, well-behaving, romantic, loving self, then the biggest roadblock in the healing of Dolly's psychological health will be removed. The thought was born after a few observations Jasmona made during rounds of discussions. Dolly used to get sudden jerks, blurry vision, hiccups, whenever Rajat was around them. She still hadn't come out of the mental shock she suffered on that unfateful day or the collective experiences throughout her life. The very presence of Rajat was creating mental trauma for her.

Because medical science has its own limits and constraints, the treatment of Dolly's paralysis could take a lot of time. Whereas, in modern medical science, it has been observed and recorded, too, that if a doctor succeeds in nullifying the stress in the patient's mind born out of diseases and, thus, winning the confidence of the patient, then half the battle is won. Then the medicines and treatments just support the body for self-recovering processes.

She concluded that the case had two patients—the wife and the husband.

Chapter 3

Plan

Jasmona's mind was working 24×7 to find foolproof solutions for Dolly's case.

Though she was responsible for the whole hospital, Dolly's case was the highest priority for her. Her credentials portray her as a high profile doctor, who had never let down expectations of patients or the management.

The cruel PAUSE in Dolly's life had to be unlocked, using the learnings from her troubled PAST, to make a foolproof PLAN to make her PLAY again.

The root causes responsible for the PAUSE were different in nature, but the master key for both seemed to be the same, lying in the basics of human psychology.

Improvement in Dolly's physical health was dependent on her mental health, and improvement in her mental health was dependent on Rajat's improved behaviour, rather reinvigoration into his old jolly, joyous, funny, pleasantly extrovert, entertaining avatar.

A lot of dots connected haphazardly here and there and after a lot of brainstorming, finally, a preliminary plan shaped up in Jasmona's mind.

Firstly, she decided to keep Dolly in ICU and not in a private ward because she wanted to maintain a distance between the wife and husband for the sake of providing better peace of mind to the wife. She also continued their long chats and talking to her children over video calls.

Secondly, she decided to ask Rajat to handle his daily routines at his own ease, but be present there only and stay in the ICU visitor's dormitory till Dolly's discharge.

One evening, Rajat got a call from Jasmona, who asked him to see her in the cabin. Rajat was surprised as he wondered what it could be about after so many days of dry behaviour from her towards him. He expected something pleasant to be there for him.

After reaching her cabin, he was further surprised to find Jasmona with her graceful smiling face. He noticed an inviting warmth in her eyes. Actually, he was starving to see her with such positive vibes towards him. He didn't doubt anything but felt emotionally satisfied after seeing Jasmona embracing his expectations.

Her very first words shocked him and his eyes widened.

Jasmona whispered in her dramatic soprano voice, "Rajat! Please sing a song for me."

Hearing such a romantic request, he choked; his face blushed like a desperately waiting lover, eyes perplexed and mind suddenly gone blank. He couldn't utter a single word.

"What happened Rajat? Don't want to sing a song for me?" Jasmona continued seducing him with her alluring voice.

"No, no. Not like that. Actually, suddenly, you want to hear a song from me just like you did years ago. I can't believe it. I haven't sung in a long time. I am confused. What is going on?"

"Do you trust me? Do you still trust me?"

"Yes. A big yes." More than his words, Rajat's eyes were showcasing his emotions.

"Then, don't question. Do what I am asking you to do. You know that I never do anything wrong." Jasmona further soothed him with her seductive voice.

"But—" Rajat was still curious.

However, Jasmona intervened. "No ifs, no buts. The time has gone for those childish excuses. Now, it's time for you to follow me if you want to come out of this situation."

"Yes, yes, definitely. I am dying to come out of this situation. It has already been two months; I am out of my office and have gotten multiple warnings from my boss. I lost my promotion as well. Please help me out of this situation, or I may lose my job, too." Rajat almost pleaded.

Jasmona realized that he was still primarily concerned about his promotion and his job, Dolly seemed to be his liability rather than responsibility.

"See, Rajat, I am sorry that you didn't get the promotion. I do feel sympathetic for you about your prospects of losing the job. But if you lose this job, you can still get a new one. But if you lose your wife, you can't get her back. So, it's better to prioritize your wife's health and wellbeing and I am the doctor of your wife, so you must listen to me."

"Ok. But I still can't understand, why do you want me to sing? How will my singing help you in treating my wife?"

"That's your biggest problem, Rajat. You unnecessarily poke your nose everywhere. You have lost many things in your life because of your ego, your adamancy, your dominating attitude, and you are still not willing to improve. Learn to listen, unlearn your own rotten convictions. Learn to trust people, unlearn to suspect your own people.

When, after so many years, I asked you to sing a song, instead of honouring my request, you are still questioning me, which means you don't trust me."

After hearing those piercing words from Jasmona, Rajat's mind started working very fast. His subconscious mind alerted him, not to take any chance, else he could lose her for the second time. He whispered apologetically, "You are right, Jasmona. Which song should I sing?" and smiled.

Jasmona felt relaxed as she finally succeeded in moulding Rajat in her way. She asked him to sing his favourite song, *"Kabhi sochta hu ki mein kuch kahu."*

Rajat started singing that song along with expressions and body movements. He got up from his chair and roamed around Jasmona while singing. On a few occasions, he enacted touching her, but she managed to keep him away. After completing the song he asked, "How was it?"

"Wah Rajat Wah! Very good! For the first attempt, you sang very nice. Though there were some issues with the voice quality and rhythms, it's ok. I am confident that you will improve with practice. Isn't it? Still, you are a rockstar." Jasmona pampered him.

As Jasmona's cabin was a huge cabin made of mirrored opaque glass, the outside was visible from inside, but the inside was not visible from outside. In addition to that, the cabin was completely soundproof, so the people inside were least bothered about the voice levels.

Meanwhile, Jasmona delegated the majority of tasks to her teams and changed her late evening schedules. All the routine work and meetings in the late evening hours were now rescheduled in the late afternoon hours.

The door was bolted from inside, displaying a Don't Disturb Board at the outer side, while spending precious time with Rajat.

The appreciation from Jasmona boosted his morale. He started singing his other favourite song, which sounded a little better.

That evening, slowly Rajat returned to his form of yesteryears and went on singing songs one after another.

After so many years, he really enjoyed himself and thought that Jasmona might also have enjoyed it in the same way as she was a huge fan of his singing. He was also thinking that, perhaps, her years-old silenced love for him might be blossoming again in her heart.

From the next day onwards, it became a routine. After the visitors' hours and then Dolly's talk sessions, Jasmona and Rajat would spend time together in her cabin, listening to Hindi filmy songs from Rajat. Day by day he was regaining a better grip over his singing.

One day, Jasmona remembered that in those days Rajat used to play mouth organ. When she requested, he immediately expressed his pleasure to play songs on the mouth organ, but they didn't have the instrument.

The next day, Jasmona bought a brand new mouth organ while coming to the hospital and gifted it to Rajat in the evening. Rajat played the instrument, which might have stolen some hearts.

After a few days, when Jasmona reminded him about his mimicry skills, Rajat performed a few mimicries, which made Jasmona laugh till tears brimmed in her eyes and her stomach started to ache.

On many occasions, while in the flow of singing and instrument playing, as per the mood of those particular songs, Rajat used to enact various romantic gestures with Jasmona, presuming her to be the actress from those songs, touching, hugging, or gesturing to kiss her. While Jasmona tactfully succeeded in avoiding Rajat's physical advances.

The daydreamer, Rajat, carrying hidden vested interests in his heart, believed that Jasmona's gestures could be common precautionary measures by any woman to safeguard her modesty against undue physical advances by any known man or stranger.

Soon they started having dinner together and, later, breakfast and lunch as well.

Whatever Jasmona was doing in public or her cabin, was pulling the attention of fellow staff, doctors, nurses, administration staff and other people. Some people were webbing and spreading spicy stories, but Jasmona was least bothered about such cheapos.

A few old sneaking tattletales, approached the owners of the hospital, complaining that the new MD was spending way more time on Dolly's case than required and lesser attention to other issues of the hospital. As per them, the working style of the new MD did not suit the Company's Policy and work culture.

However, the management saw a different picture. When they investigated the case, they felt proud of their decision to select Dr Dave as their MD. The clandestine investigation reports highlighted that Dolly's case was critically unique and historically severest. Data indicated that, historically, the survival rate in such cases was almost 0%. The complainers lost their faces as their complaint was found biased and insanely attention-hungry.

What Dr Jasmona was doing was surprisingly appreciable. She had an innovative plan in implementation to treat Dolly, not only for recovery from the current additional health issues of neurological, paralytic, nervous breakdown issues but for a permanent recovery against the severe menopausal disorders. She wanted to make this case a milestone case for India and the world, where women suffering from such severe menopausal disorders could be successfully treated to make them survive and help them lead a normal healthy life in the post-menopause phase. She was confident of her innovative treatment method and hopeful that, later on, the City Hospital would be a pioneer in such treatments.

The secret investigation team couldn't find the details of the treatments for Dolly's case. However, they got the hint that, in future, the treatments of such cases couldn't be generic but would be case-specific with varied methods, where the core principles of treatment methods would be based on basic human values interlinked with their DNA imprint.

Based on secret inquiries with several patients, their relatives, hospital staff, vendors, the investigation teams also found that Dr Jasmona was very fast in making decisions and implementing actions compared to other senior-level doctors in other hospitals. That's why she could finish the routine tasks at a very high speed compared to others. Many more positive feedbacks about Jasmona made the management happy.

A lot of action was going on in Dolly's case. The routine medical treatments for neurological issues and memory disorders; three-time physiotherapy for paralysis; balancing the hormonal deficiencies caused by menopausal transformations; enhancing hormonal levels, immunity and energy levels; treatments for joint soreness and stiffness, heart functions, dizziness, skin irritations, urinary disorders, hot flashes, anxiety, depression, nervous breakdown symptoms and mood swings; and weight management, etc. Jasmona managed to put high-level experts for each health issue.

Jasmona was building a close personal relationship with her instead of a formal doctor-patient relationship, making her talk more and open up, video calling her children, making her laugh and smile despite the tracheostomy in the neck. Jasmona was trying to make her happy and provide her with the old happy and healthy life.

Dolly would eagerly wait for Jasmona to come and meet her. Her anxiety, bad mood, depression, restlessness and heavy head vanished as soon as she saw Jasmona. Dolly's condition was improving day after day and she was reinstating the spirit of living.

The only hitch was observed whenever Rajat came into the picture or she heard his voice. Her face would lose its normalcy, eyes lost the glitter, throat choked, lips locked together. Jasmona observed those symptoms many many times, which inspired her additional innovative plan for treating Dolly.

Jasmona was managing Rajat's daily practice of singing, playing the mouth organ and mimicries without fail. Not only the practice of various art forms, but gradually, people started finding him well-behaved. He would smile and talk nicely. The reasons behind these transformations may be different for Jasmona and others, but for Rajat, the reasons were quite surprising and insane.

Rajat had fallen in love again. Surprisingly, with his old, once silenced love, Jasmona. He was trapped once again, under the mesmerizing womanish influence of Jasmona's overall magnetic persona, her sweet behaviour, her emotional traits, her frequent advances during art practices. Even at the age of 55, having spent a married life of 30 years, an ailing bedridden wife and married children, he was once again blindly in love with Jasmona.

The old saying "Love is Blind" was not relevant in this case, but the saying "Men will be men" was true up to a significant extent. Because, of late, it has been observed in societies, despite all the odds, there are 99% chances that males may intend for extra marital affairs or start having relations outside of marriage if the lady is misunderstood for her unintentional courtesies.

The Deputy Managing Director, known as highly egoist, adamant, motor-mouthed and a man with heavy head weight, was surprisingly obeying Jasmona like a schoolboy. Though Jasmona was understanding Rajat's expectations from her, she was least bothered and very much focussed on her own plan. On a few occasions, Jasmona thought to explain her plan to Rajat in micro details but dropped the idea, as it might have distracted him from doing what was expected from him.

Chapter 4

Played

The wheel of time continued rotating endlessly, without waiting for anybody.

Five months passed in the hospital. Dolly had improved significantly well. However, a few deficiencies were still being observed occasionally. The major issues were breathlessness, sudden oxygen deficiency, low energy levels, calcium deficiency, vitamin deficiencies, rising creatinine levels, inconsistent blood pressure, mild convulsions, etc. All this was happening out of post-menopause hormonal imbalances and neurological instabilities.

The major factor was womanhood oriented, where the body stops the production of reproduction supporting hormones immediately after attaining menopause. The absence of those hormones causes cascading effects on the overall functions of the body. As her case was diagnosed as severe menopause, utmost care was required during the ongoing holistic treatments.

The improvements achieved so far were gradually building the confidence of Jasmona, mainly the paralysis was healed up to a significant extent, where she regained sensations and movements in the right side of her body, minimum basic brain functions and vital functions, neurological stability in favourable environments, speaking efficiency and growing will power.

Observing the progress, Jasmona consulted expert doctors and as per their advice decided to remove the tracheostomy and allowed Dolly to receive oral feeding for selective drinkable items like water, milk, tea, juices, etc., and liquefied food items. She wanted Dolly to achieve significant progress at oral feeding.

Jasmona decided to discharge her from the hospital, though ICU conditions at home were required because her health needed to be monitored closely. Because of the complexities of her case, dependency over life-support machines could arise at any point in time, like nebulization, oxygen concentrator, portable ventilator and necessary supporting feeds like saline, IV fluids, etc.

Dolly was very happy returning home but was equally upset as she would miss Jasmona. Jasmona assured her that she would visit her daily. Both Dolly and Rajat were unaware of Jasmona's plan.

Meanwhile, Jasmona convinced Akshay and Anjali to not visit their mother unless she allows them. Their untimely visit could disturb her plan to heal their mother. Till then, she would continue to let Dolly video call them.

By that time Dolly and Rajat had become grandparents, Akshay & his wife were blessed with a baby girl, Anjali & her husband were blessed with a baby boy. As usual, Anjali and Akshay were rarely calling Rajat, and Rajat never called them after their last call.

Before finalizing her PLAN, Jasmona properly assessed Rajat's financial health. Being at a senior corporate position for many years, Rajat was financially sound and had cleared the medical bills through the health insurance he had availed for Dolly.

Rajat had lost his job. After three months of absence from his office, he was asked to resign. No mercy was shown for such a great contributor of the organization. He was replaced by some other aspirant down the line in hierarchy. Disgusted, Rajat cursed his organization for the ill-treatment at such a critical phase of his life. But things were not in his control, so he silently processed the exit formalities. Now, he was left with only one job—taking care of his bed-ridden wife.

Jasmona sympathized with him but, at the same time, couldn't stop herself from saying, "Whatever happens in life, happens for good reasons. So, don't worry and get ready to win the future."

Jasmona helped Rajat in setting up ICU at home in a dedicated room for Dolly, by providing the best agency for supply, installation, operation and maintenance of all ICU equipment, timely supply of medicines and consumables, 24x7 Nursing Services. Two senior nurses were selected by Jasmona and stationed there for round the clock nursing. She arranged visits of all expert doctors, technicians and physiotherapists similar to the hospital schedules. She arranged to install IP based CCTV Cameras in and outside the house, which enabled her to watch the live display and recorded footage.

After a satisfactory setup of ICU and deputation of nurses at home, Jasmona called a kick-off meeting with Rajat and the nurses to brief her plan. She requested everyone not to interrupt at any point in time and ask questions at the end of the meeting.

The very first activity in the morning, Rajat has to serve the morning bed tea to Dolly as he was doing 30 years ago when they started their life together as a newly married couple, full of mutual love and desire. Rajat will have to enact the same madly loving husband with the then body language, gestures and expressions to ensure a happy beginning of the day for Dolly. Similarly, Rajat has to serve the evening tea with her favourite snacks.

After the morning tea, the nurses have to do all the daily routine morning courses for her including sponging, checking & recording all the parameters and ensuring that Dolly takes her medicines.

Then, Rajat has to help Dolly with breathing exercises, Pranayama and yoga practices as per the Yoga Chart prepared by Jasmona.

Then, Rajat has to take Dolly out for a morning walk-cum-wheelchair ride over the walkers' track and nearby community garden. One nurse has to accompany them for any unforeseen emergency, but Rajat has to steer the wheelchair. Rajat has to ensure a minimum 5 km walk, and it has to be increased with time as per Dolly's stamina. During the morning walk, Rajat has to ensure smiles and laughs for Dolly's face by cracking jokes enacting comically, enabling her to memorize those old golden moments of life, when she laughed a lot or smiled a lot. The nurse has to make the videos, which Jasmona will watch later.

Then, Rajat has to take Dolly to the Laughter Club, to provide her with exposure to the galaxy of laughter, happiness and absorbing healthy positive vibes out of the healthiest and happiest ambience.

Then, after returning home, after shower/sponging, Rajat has to accompany her for the morning course of Pooja rituals.

Then, Rajat has to prepare a breakfast of Dolly's choice out of the Diet Chart prepared by the dietician. The nurse has to complete the basic preparations of raw materials for the breakfast. Then, Rajat has to feed the breakfast to Dolly with his own hands, with emotions like a loving husband feeds an ailing wife or a mother feeds her child.

After breakfast, as per Dolly's wish, either Rajat has to do read the newspaper to her or watch the TV. If at any point in time she needs rest, then let her rest or sleep for a while.

Then Rajat has to accompany the visiting doctors, physiotherapists and technicians for thorough check-ups and routine tests.

The masseur has to give a massage to Dolly twice a day. The nurses have to accompany the masseur.

The physiotherapist has to conduct exercise sessions twice a day.

Then, before lunch, Rajat has to host a very special session for at least an hour. He has to sing songs or play the mouth organ or do mimicry acts as per Dolly's wishes. Rajat has to ensure performing all these activities as he was doing for Dolly in the early years of their marriage, with the same energy levels, emotions, expressions, gestures, romantic traits. Dolly should be asked for her comment on the quality of performance. Jasmona would also keep track of Rajat's performances. Nurses have to capture the pics and make videos of Rajat's performances, which she would be watching later to see her emotional recoveries.

Those words shocked Rajat and then he understood the secret behind those art practice sessions. During those sessions, he was under the impression that she was asking to do all those activities out of her sweet memories of yesteryears when they were together and in love with each other. At the same time, he also understood that Jasmona had cleverly managed to know from Dolly many secrets of their life, specifically about him. Precisely about the darker sides of his character.

The saying of wise old people "Love is blind," proved true. He did fall in love with Jasmona again and did everything she wanted him to do without even thinking about the reason behind it. He had never imagined that she would play so tactfully, finding out the truth from two different sources and using him as a pawn in her game plan.

He thought of finding out ways to counter Jasmona's double-crossing. However, nothing could be done, as everything was under her control, and he had lost his job. Any wrong move could jeopardize his life further. He could lose Dolly and would have to suffer a lonely painful life. He couldn't afford to lose his wife, at any cost, at this stage of life.

But, parallelly, a few self-criticising questions, too, were challenging him. What wrong had she done by double-crossing them? Whatever she did, as a professional doctor, was for the best possible healing of Dolly. So, what's wrong with it?

He realized his own feelings of one-sided love towards her were insanely delusional. His expectation, to win back her love after all those years, was out of his own vested interests. As a shrewd chance-catcher, he was trying to get into an extramarital affair. He fell for his own perverted intentions of infidelity. He decided to stop blaming Jasmona for her good unselfish deeds and to fulfil the expectations of her PLAN.

Finally, Rajat got self-convinced and geared up for Jasmona's PLAN, but while self-talking he was appearing disturbed and distracted. Jasmona noticed and asked, "Is anything wrong, Rajat?"

"No! I was just thinking how I can do all your tasks in the best possible manner?" Rajat replied as a glib liar, hiding the real turbulence going on in his mind.

"Ok, guys. Let's resume the briefing," Jasmona said smilingly. "So, after the recreational entertaining sessions, lunch has to be served to Dolly by Rajat. Like breakfast, Rajat will feed Dolly with his own hands. The major preparation of lunch will be done by Rajat, in line with the Diet Chart.

After lunch, nurses will feed the medicines, and then, Rajat will take out Dolly for a 30-minute wheel-chair ride and keep on entertaining her with his jokes and comic acts.

After that, it will be rest time for Dolly.

After her waking up in the late afternoon or evening, it will be the time for her evening tea and snacks served by Rajat.

Then, the massage session and physiotherapy session and intermittent observation of various health parameters like BP, oxygen, temperature, pulse rate, etc., will be recorded regularly.

After that, it will be time for the evening session of recreational entertainment. Rajat has to perform singing, mouth organ playing, mimicries, etc., for one hour.

Then, Rajat has to feed Dolly dinner in line with the Diet Chart. Like breakfast and lunch, the major preparation of dinner has to be done by Rajat.

Then nurses will have to ensure feeding of medicines and recording of health parameters. Post-dinner, Rajat has to take Dolly out for a wheel-chair ride and keep on entertaining her with his jokes and comic acts.

Then, the time for night sleep for Dolly. One nurse has to be consistently present near Dolly during the sleeping hours.

After waking up in the morning, the same routine has to be followed.

In nutshell, apart from daily routines of nursing care and medical processes, Rajat has to ensure two sessions of sharing tea, feeding breakfast, lunch and dinner with his own hands, three sessions of wheel-chair rides and two sessions of recreational entertainment. Though the majority of activities will be recorded in CCTV cameras, we will also have to record pictures and videos for future references and analysis. At the same time, we have to record and analyse the amount of laughter in minutes for each entertainment session every day."

Rajat had to play the most important role in this plan, where he had to pour in emotions to the fullest. He had to transform himself into the same madly loving husband similar to those initial golden years after their marriage. He must mould Dolly to trust that she got back the same romantic loving husband, lovable by people around, with pleasant personality as always smiling, who is funny, versatile singer, nice music instrument player, mimicry & comic actor, laughter rioter, a delight to have in life.

"And one more thing, Rajat, you will have to strictly quit smoking and drinking, else you can't win her trust and consequentially her treatments will be jeopardized," warned Jasmona.

Rajat intervened, "But, I already quit smoking and drinking six months ago while I was in the hospital.

"Don't lie, Rajat. I don't know about drinking, but you are still smoking. The peculiar smell of tobacco always comes from your mouth and your clothes. Please, this is my humble request in the name of Dolly and a strict instruction as a doctor; quit smoking forever, if you want to see your wife alive."

The shameless liar in Rajat understood the heat of the issue and surrendered. "Ok, done."

"Let me tell you that Dolly's case requires mental treatment and emotional treatment more than the conventional medical treatment. Regaining a strong emotional quotient is the most essential primary need of her personality, in addition to the improvements in her physical health. I will be closely monitoring the progress of Dolly's recovery, and I will be visiting Dolly regularly. Now, best of luck guys, the action starts now."

The execution of Jasmona's plan started very well. Everything was happening smoothly.

People, who knew Rajat, couldn't recognize him. A miraculous transformation had taken place of a tough nut into a soft lovable guy, whose innocent smile could change the ambience and encourage others to smile.

The very first morning, Dolly couldn't believe it when Rajat greeted her pleasantly with a melodious "Good Morning." She was further surprised when he offered her tea made by him. She couldn't believe it and wondered if she was dreaming. She thought if it was real or had the clock reversed by many years.

Hesitantly, while looking into his eyes inquisitively with mixed emotions, she took the cup in her left hand. The very first sip of the tea made Dolly emotional, as she remembered the taste. She whispered, "Oh, Rajat! You made this tea for me?"

"Yes, Dolly. From now on, I will make tea for you. You like it?"

"Yes. Yes. I love it. I missed this taste all these years."

"Now, everything will be set right like before." He sat with her in a half-hug posture on the reclined bed, which comforted Dolly with emotions. "Dolly, now you freshen up, I will come back to you later. Ok?"

Dolly was perplexed, she couldn't believe that she had witnessed such a nice beginning of the morning, just like it used to happen many years ago in the initial days after their marriage.

After she had freshened up, Rajat helped Dolly get on the wheelchair and brought her to the living hall. "Dolly, now let's do some exercises. I will demonstrate and guide you. Would you like to do the same?" Rajat asked with great enthusiasm

Dolly wondered what the hell was going on. First the morning tea, then Rajat sat with her. It seemed to her that her illness had changed him. She replied, "Yes! I will do. I like yoga."

"Ok, Madam. So, now the yoga classes start. Let me introduce myself. I am Rajat Guruji, your yoga teacher. Now, let's begin," Rajat comically said.

Dolly laughed. "Yes Sir."

Rajat started with light breathing exercises like Anulom Vilom, Bhastrika, Bhramari, Udgeet and Kapaal Bhati.

Dolly didn't feel any difficulty in doing Anulom Vilom. As her right side was still not 100% functional, so, she used her left hand for alternate nostril breathing. Rajat observed that her healed-up right-side paralysis was no more an obstacle for her to inhale & exhale from the right nostril.

She also did Bhastrika without any problem. She was comfortable in inhaling together with both nostrils and then exhaling from both nostrils together, which meant that the right side paralysis was healed.

Udgeet was also done satisfactorily.

However, while doing Bhramari, she needed Rajat's help, who used his right hand to cover her eye and ear, and then Dolly did it successfully.

While doing Kapaal Bhati, Dolly felt pain in her abdomen, as she was unable to sync the exhale of breath and the abdominal movement together. So, Rajat dropped the idea of practising Kapaal Bhati for now and convinced her to start doing it after a few days, when she would be able to do it.

Overall, Dolly felt very good while doing breathing exercises.

Then, Rajat guided her to do light exercises using palms, hands, feet, legs and shoulders while she sat in the wheelchair as she couldn't stand on her own for long durations.

So, after 30 minutes of yoga and exercise sessions, Rajat expressed joyously, "So, Madam! How was the yoga session? I found you did very well."

"Yes Sir! I enjoyed it. I want to do it again," Dolly also responded in a joyful manner.

"Ok, Madam! So, now we will be doing some more interesting activities. Let's move," Rajat yelled in a comical manner and drove the wheelchair outside. One nurse followed them.

On the very first day, Rajat was managing very well while comically presenting himself with loads of love but maintaining the suspense for the next course of surprises.

During the wheelchair ride, Rajat cracked jokes, few were new and few were very old which he shared with her many years back. Dolly couldn't control her laughter and laughed madly all the way. Naughty Rajat cracked a couple of non-veg jokes while the nurse was away from them. Dolly listened and laughed with shy expressions.

After walking to-and-fro for 5 km, Rajat took her to a nearby community garden, where Laughter Club's routine laughter sessions were being conducted. It was free for everybody and no membership or registration process was required to join. Coincidentally, they reached in time and joined one of the sessions, which had just started. The ambience there was filled with a variety of thunderous laughter waves in quite natural ways one-after-another. Dolly tried to laugh and match the frequencies and rhythms.

After that laughter session, they returned home.

The nurses gave a sponge bath to Dolly, dressed her and brought her to the living room. Rajat also reached there, after he had taken a shower and took Dolly to the pooja room. He parked her wheelchair resting there and started lighting Diyas. Dolly was finding everything unbelievable because she had never seen Rajat initiating such holy routines at home.

Then Rajat started chanting the Mantras, which Dolly used to chant daily before the hospitalization. When Dolly saw Rajat chanting holy mantras for her, loads of emotions poured through her heart and tears brimmed in her eyes. She also started chanting in unison with Rajat.

After the Mantras, Rajat gave a bell to Dolly and started chanting Aartis. Dolly started ringing the bell while chanting Aartis with Rajat.

Finally, after a soulful completion of Pooja, Rajat brought Dolly to the dining hall. He asked her to wait there and said that he would be back in ten minutes.

"Now, Madam, it's time for breakfast, and today the chef has prepared your favourite breakfast. Guess what is it?" Rajat comically said in chef's getup while driving the trolley carrying breakfast and utensils.

"Kanda Poha," Dolly delightedly said.

"But how can you guys forget me? Kanda Poha is my favourite, too." A pleasant voice pulled their attention.

"Oh. Dr Dave. We can never forget you. I was just arranging everything and then would have waited for you. But you are very very punctual. You reached here on dot," Rajat kept on saying in his comical tone.

"Yes, Di. We were waiting for you." Dolly confirmed Rajat's words.

"Ok. Ok. I know. Now, let's have breakfast. Then, I have to rush to the hospital," Jasmona comforted them.

When Jasmona saw that Rajat was feeding Dolly from his own hands, she smiled and gestured to him with thanks.

They talked briefly while having breakfast, and then Jasmona left for the hospital.

After breakfast, Rajat brought Dolly to the living room and started reading out updates from her favourite newspapers. Then he switched on the television and surfed a few of her favourite channels.

After the newspaper and television sessions, Rajat told Dolly that soon five doctors would be visiting one-after-another and that he would also be there. Jasmona had planned the doctors' morning visits before they went to the hospital. After the doctor's visits, the masseur would visit for massaging the body. Then the physiotherapist would come.

After the completion of massage and physiotherapy sessions, nurses brought Dolly to the living hall and left. Dolly was looking for Rajat, but he was not there. A few moments passed, there was no movement in the living hall. Lonely Dolly started feeling uncomfortable, and when she was just about to call Rajat out, she heard something.

"Pal bhar ke liye koi hame pyar kar le, jhootha hi sahi…" The sweet words from one of her favourite songs poured into her ears from nowhere. She sensed that it was Rajat's voice. She remembered he used to sing this song years ago. She couldn't see Rajat, only his voice was audible.

"Do din ke liye koi ekrar kar le, jootha hi sahi…" The melody continued. Anxious Dolly swung her eyes all around, moving her head here and there. Her blood pressure was rising under blown-up emotions.

Suddenly, somebody covered her eyes from behind and the melody continued, *"Hamne bahot tujhko chup chup ke dekha…"* and when her eyes were uncovered, she blushed like a new bride.

It was Rajat, who was singing her favourite song, not exactly in the original play-back voice, but in his own raw uncultured voice. He was not only singing but acting, too. Holding Dolly's face in his hands, kissing intermittently, he continued singing and kept on changing the postures, gestures and body language.

Meanwhile, Dolly was just frozen amidst such shockingly surprising comic moments full of intermingled strings of varied emotions. Her lips were frozen like icebergs, tears of happiness frozen like tiny ice balls in her widened eyes, cheeks reddened more than red, goosebumps over her body, not fading away.

After completion of the song, Rajat sat on his knees and hugged her very tightly. Dolly couldn't control her emotions and cried out as she got back her lost love. Seeing her tears, Rajat whispered again melodiously, *"Dekh sakta hu mai kuch bhi hote hue, nahi mai nahi dekh sakta tujhe rote hue…"*

Although this song was originally sung by a brother for her sad sister. An old wise saying suggests that a woman mustn't be left crying helplessly. Whether she is a mother, sister, daughter, lover, wife, friend, any relative, or even any stranger, never do anything unwanted, unacceptable, unagreeable, unpleasant to her or hurting her dignity, modesty, self-respect, which could hurt her heart and could bring tears in her eyes because it's not her tears, it's indirectly Nature's tears.

So, Rajat kept on singing, fulfilling her emotional hunger, making her feel as her prince charming has returned. After that song, Rajat changed the art form. He started playing mimicries of many famous personalities. Not exactly in the same voice and mannerisms but somewhat funny and enjoyable.

From the sea of emotions, Dolly, now, found herself in the valleys of crazy laughter. She laughed till her stomach started aching.

Rajat then stopped doing comedy and asked, "Madam! Now, which song do you want to listen to?"

"*Ae meri zoharaa zabi,*" Dolly shyly wished.

"Oh! Wah wah madam! What a choice," Rajat comically enacted and started singing the song.

The entertainment session went the most emotional and hilarious way. One of the nurses kept on recording all the movements from the best possible hidden angles. Meanwhile, Jasmona also watched a few chunks of that session and felt very happy.

Thereafter, Rajat brought her to the dining hall and started preparations for serving lunch. Meanwhile, Jasmona joined them. Rajat served the lunch that he prepared during the visits of the masseur and physiotherapist. Jasmona kept her eye on Rajat, but he didn't let her down and started feeding Dolly with his own hands. Jasmona left for the hospital after lunch.

Post lunch medications, Rajat again took Dolly for 30 minutes wheelchair ride and entertained her by cracking jokes and a few naughty comical acts. Then after the wheelchair ride session, Rajat brought Dolly back to her reclined bed in the home ICU and helped her lie comfortably and have rest, as she was feeling a little sleepy.

When Dolly opened her eyes, she found one nurse waiting for her to wake up, who then greeted her by wishing good evening. The nurse helped her freshen up. Meanwhile, Rajat came with evening tea and snacks. He served the tea and fed her snacks. Dolly felt so pleased having such a nice beginning of the evening hours.

Then Rajat told that now she would have evening sessions of massage and physiotherapy and he would come back later. One of the nurses would be present there with her during the evening sessions.

After those sessions, the nurse brought her to the living hall. Dolly's eyes were searching for Rajat, who dramatically surfaced singing lines from famous Hindi filmy songs. One-after-another he kept on singing songs of Dolly's wish. He played songs on the mouth organ too, which made her enormously happy. He enacted a few mimicries, too, which left Dolly in pools of laughter.

Post that recreational session, Rajat brought Dolly to the dining hall and started arrangements for serving the dinner. As committed, Jasmona also joined them. They enjoyed the dinner prepared and served by Rajat, who was doing this for the first time in his life. Jasmona didn't skip watching Rajat feeding Dolly with his own hands.

Post dinner, Jasmona, Rajat and Dolly spent a little time together. While walking together for some time, they discussed the day's happenings. Jasmona was cautiously noticing Dolly's words, reactions, emotions, body language and level of enthusiasm around Rajat. She was quite satisfied with the results of her experiment on the very first day. It seemed that Dolly was more than happy after getting back her husband with old sweet mannerisms, a sense of caring and an entertaining persona. She didn't forget to video call Akshay and Anjali. Rajat also spoke a little.

All were happy at the end of the day. Jasmona bid goodbye with a promise of joining the next day for breakfast.

The nurses fed Dolly with the night course of medications and recorded all the health parameters. They didn't forget to send all the pictures and videos recorded that day.

Then Rajat, sitting beside Dolly, massaged her hands and muttered a few music pieces randomly. He suddenly started singing a lullaby as if Dolly were a baby feeling sleepy. After a few minutes of singing, Dolly went into a deep sleep.

Rajat left Dolly to one of the nurses, who would be attending her in the night shift.

Day 1 was wonderfully satisfactory for everyone.

The next day and every day thereafter, a lot of betterment and improvement happened in terms of all the parameters involved in Dolly's case.

Rajat's artistic and dramatic performances bettered with time. In addition to that, the rejuvenation of his overall persona, the art of presenting oneself, body language, behavioural science, treatment to people around, the art of self-restraint, the down to earth attitude, listening habits and many more positivities were now recognitions of his improved personality. Apart from that, Rajat also earned back the lovability in his ailing wife's heart, which was lost many years ago. The wife who, just a few days back, seemed to be afraid of Rajat's presence or who used to get nervous hearing his voice, was now wishing her husband to be always with her.

One more unconventional, peculiarly surprising, thing happened, nowadays Dolly was often seeing Rajat in her dreams while sleeping. She used to dream about him and his pleasant traits and coquetry only. Whatever she used to watch and enjoy during the day with her open eyes, almost the replica of the same she used to dream about. Sometimes she dreamt of running with him, which she couldn't in real life, in farms, jungles, gardens and beaches. Sometimes of naughty Rajat's physical advances for intimacy and many more dreamy dreams. It was making her sleep pleasant. Whenever she got up, she was always carrying a stress-free jovial mood.

So, the positivities of Rajat was influencing the all-round development of mental and physical positivities in Dolly.

Around seven days later, she started walking using a walker. After a few more days' practice, she started walking using a walking stick. After a few more days, she started walking independently, however, with intermittent support from Rajat or nurses. She started performing her daily routines and moved around independently.

Her daily routine check-ups for various physical, vital parameters showed satisfactory improvements in her system. Her routine weekly, bi-weekly and monthly special check-ups for sensitive parameters for post paralytic improvements, the health of the brain after the operation for blood clots, memory functions, speech functions, menopause oriented physical and psychological/hormonal balancing and enhancements, neurological parameters, IQ, EQ, immunity enhancement and few more important aspects were showing satisfactory improvements. Now she was almost out of the physical & psychological dangers caused by the dual threats of severest menopause and half-paralysis.

Dolly had transformed completely. She not only recovered from the deadly menopause and paralysis but also regained the entity as the wife full of love and devotion towards her husband and childish instincts at the bottom of her heart.

Jasmona's plan worked, where in addition to the conventional modern-day medical science and treatment technologies, she used alternative treatments targeting basic human instincts and Emotional Quotient to revamp and connect the burnt bridges between suffered womanhood and dominating adamant patriarchy. Prima facie, it seemed that she successfully resolved the issue with an innovative blend of IQ, EQ and SQ and executed a healthy mind game between the wife and husband.

After witnessing the successful implementation of her plan for three months and being satisfied with the latest reports highlighting the desired improvements, Jasmona decided to take the plan to the next level by making Dolly's case more inspirational. She decided to set up various indoor and outdoor sports in their bungalow.

The daily chats introduced Jasmona to Dolly's favourite games/sports, which she either used to play or loved to watch. So, without losing time, arrangements had been made for Dolly to practice sprinting on 100 m, 200 m, tracks made at the community sports ground. In the lawn area of the house, arrangements had been made for Badminton, Basket Ball, Table Tennis, Football, Cricket and inside the house for Carrom Board and Chess. Though all those sports were available virtually, Jasmona preferred real lively games.

So, now Jasmona rescheduled the whole plan and revised the diet chart. Now, Dolly was in need of food for enhancing physical strength, stamina and immunity.

Apart from the existing activities of the earlier plan, the practices for new activities for the revised plan started with full enthusiasm, warmth, drive, determination, dynamism, zest and passion.

Dolly and Rajat were recharged with the latest successes at her health conditions and truly felt obliged to Jasmona. They had mentally prepared themselves to do or die but never let down Jasmona.

After a few days of practice, it was found that Dolly was doing much better at sprinting. All the other sports would take much more time getting tuned into as hands and legs synchronization was required.

Jasmona decided to give priority to sprinting rather than longer spell running and to schedule more time for it. She decided to give lesser priority to other sports. However, indoor games like carrom board and chess must be played daily.

As the time passed, surprisingly, Dolly's efficiency at running was improving day-by-day, in terms of stamina, level of interest, distance run per spell and time durations. Jasmona was very much excited at her experiment, which she braved with calculated risks. Rajat was also very much satisfied at observing Dolly's newborn enthusiasm in life. And what could be said about Dolly; she was running on dream tracks, which she had never dreamt of in her wild dreams.

After some time, Dolly started running on roadside jogging tracks, and poor Rajat had to follow her, which he was doing by merely walking. Sometimes, Jasmona also joined them, when time permitted.

Three months had passed. Now, Dolly, the 51-year-old lady, a survivor of severest menopause, paralysis and brain injury, was running 5 km per day at a moderate speed.

One fine day, after the running session, while doing breakfast, Jasmona shared an advertisement for the Marathon Tournament, scheduled the next month.

"Dolly, I want you to run in this Marathon," Jasmona shocked Dolly and Rajat.

"But, she is just a beginner and has just started a few months ago. She recently survived the severe ailments. I think it will be risky," Rajat intervened.

"Oh, Rajat! Wow! I am glad to see your emotional concerns for your wife. But, don't forget I am her doctor and know her health concerns and constraints more than you. I am worried about her wellness more than you. So, don't challenge my decisions," annoyed Jasmona responded bluntly.

To cut short a possible unpleasant argument, Dolly interrupted, "I will run. I will play."

"Wow! That's the spirit. That's the strong woman. That's the iron lady. That's the fearless tigress." Happy Jasmona clapped and cheered Dolly's brave fearless response and gave a grim look to Rajat.

"But, running 25 km, don't you think it could be fatal," Rajat intervened again.

"Oye duffer! I am not asking for 25 km. She can run the half marathon of 5 km category." Jasmona cleared the air

"Oh! Ok," Rajat responded in agreement.

"Now, you both, listen carefully. We have one month, I am going to arrange a trainer as soon as possible, who will train Dolly with special techniques to compete in the half-marathon. After all, it's a matter of beating hundreds or thousands of competitors. There Dolly won't be running alone."

"Yes! I will learn well in the training," cheerful Dolly yelled.

All laughed at Dolly's childish joyousness and clapped for morale-boosting.

Fortunately, Jasmona could connect with one of the best trainers available in the city, Ms Usha Rani. The trainer was an expert dietician also.

From the very next day, Dolly's training started. Apart from training, Usha and Dolly shared a lot of personal things, too, which helped in better mutual gelling.

For the very first week, it was a morning schedule. After observing the progress and health conditions of Dolly, Usha and Jasmona decided on two training sessions per day.

Rajat always accompanied Dolly, while the training schedules.

Meanwhile, Jasmona processed all the procedures for the registration of Dolly as a participant in the half-marathon.

A month passed by and the D-Day arrived.

It was Sunday, so, Jasmona was present for the whole duration of the half marathon, scheduled to begin at 5:30 am from Bandra Fort Garden. She, herself, was all geared up for the morale-boosting of Dolly. After all, it was not only Dolly for whom this marathon mattered, but, as a doctor, that incident mattered much more for Jasmona, whose patient was going through an acid test. Jasmona was a highly positive person but, at the same time, damn practical, too. She had already made up her mind about how to handle the situation if Dolly fails and if Dolly wins then how to milk the opportunity in its fullest form. However, she was confident that whatever result will come out in a few hours, she would have the last laugh.

Meanwhile, the trainer, Usha Rani, was also present there full time. Not to support Dolly but to win the marathon. She was carrying nutrients, juices and water in her bag and would be running on a parallel track to keep a close eye on Dolly while running.

Rajat was also there to support his wife. After all, it was the very first marathon when somebody from the family was participating. However, he was a little bit confused about maintaining close proximity with Dolly while running, because, he couldn't run. Thanks to all his bad habits throughout his life. Then he decided to maintain a speedy brisk walk while Dolly would be running there in the tracks amid a crowd of thousands of competitors.

Dolly carefully listened to Usha Rani while warming up practising at the venue. Her eyes wandered all around to have a practical idea about the world moving around her, intermittently capturing glimpses of her supportive husband and her treasure of inspiration, Jasmona. The previous night, Akshay and Anjali wished her luck for the marathon and begged to gift them a win.

Finally, all participants took their positions. The sound of fire cracked the ambience. The flock of competitors moved within a fraction of a millisecond. Watching their body language while running, it was easy to recognize an amateur and a professional.

Dolly started very smoothly and was maintaining consistent speed but that did not seem sufficient to keep oneself in the competition. Her subconscious mind was continuously signalling her that she was not running as a sole runner in her society's jogger track but was in a competition and that her near and dear ones expect her to win in any condition.

Usha Rani was consistently running parallel to her in the outer track and yelling intermittently. "Dolly! Dolly! Dolly! Come on, Dolly. Come on, Dolly."

After some time, Usha sensed that approximately 1 km was covered in one/fifth time by Dolly, but still, she was way behind compared to 50% of the fellow competitors. Usha started feeling a bit desperate and started screaming, "Run, Dolly. Run, Dolly, Run. Run fast. Run fast."

Usha observed some improvements, Dolly was recovering, leaving many competitors behind her, but she was still far away from the front line runners. Usha started shouting, "Fly, Dolly, Fly. Fly, Dolly, Fly. Fly for Akshay. Fly for Anjali. Fly for Rajat. Fly, Dolly, Fly."

Hearing those words, Dolly's speed geared up to the top gear. Now she was behind the front line runners of professional sprinters. She had to go much faster to get into the front line.

Desperate Usha yelled again, "Fly, Dolly, Fly. Fly for Suraj. Fly for Sita. Fly Fly Fly."

Though Dolly was absolutely focussed on running and her eyes were on track, Usha's words were audible to her. Hearing the names of grandson, Suraj and granddaughter, Sita, her emotions erupted, legs got in sync with the whole body, which started leaping. A few seconds later, Usha was surprised to see that now Dolly was ahead of everyone. There was still 2.5 km to be covered.

Usha didn't stop boosting her morale. She kept on charging. "Fly, Dolly, Fly. Fly. Fly. Fly."

After a few milliseconds, what Usha saw shocked her to cries amid tears. The superfast running queen, Dolly, suddenly tumbled down on the track.

Dolly couldn't understand what happened and darkness surrounded her. Her subconscious mind was rigorously triggering signals to get up immediately and start running, but at the same time, she was also feeling as if she was dying.

Usha was roaring, "Get up, Dolly. Get up. Get up. Get up for Rajat. Run, Dolly. Run. Run. Come on, Dolly. Get up you champion. Get up."

Despite dying senses, Dolly was trying to come up, trying to get up, whereas the competitors were not bothered about their colleague and continued running towards the destination.

"Me no pause, me play! Me no pause, me play! Me no pause, me play! Me no pause, me play!"

When those loud riveting words pierced Dolly's ears, her eyes blinked, neurons charged with loads of signals, her body energized with tons of mental energy, her hands and legs activated and she got up. The inspiring loud words again refracted in the ambience.

"Me no pause, me play! Me Play! Me Play! Me Play! Me Play! Me Play! Me no pause, me play! Me no pause, me play! Me Play! Me Play! Me Play!"

Within a fraction of a second, Dolly's head turned towards her side. A smile sparkled over her face when she saw Jasmona shouting, waving & punching hands crazily in the air, banging her legs on the ground.

Eye contact for a few milliseconds with Jasmona exploded the unquenched fire inside her and made her shout. "Yes! I will not pause! I will play. I will play. Me no pause, me play!" Dolly shouted with all her might and vigour.

She turned her head to the front and started running like the fastest creature on earth. It was not Dolly, it was her soul fuelled by Jasmona with the fuel of never-say-die inspiring emotions.

People around, including Rajat, were surprised. The way Jasmona yelled, her words were Greek & Latin for everybody around. Even a few people were confused by the way Usha was inspiring Dolly.

She was approximately midway. Many were ahead of Dolly, beating her by a maximum by half a kilometre. The unruly, reinless, unrestrained, invisible creature inside Dolly was now ought to break all the myths. Millisecond by millisecond, second by second, the scenario in the canvas of track was changing very fast. Dolly was leaving behind the competitors one-after-another. 4 km had been covered so far, still a couple of competitors were running ahead of her.

"Me no pause, me play! Me Play! Me Play! Me Play!" Those miraculous words resonated in her ears again. Though she was focussed on the destination—hazily visible at that point of time—the sixth sense confirmed the presence of Jasmona nearby. Top-up by the soul energy booster, now the creature inside her left running, rather started flying like the fastest bird on earth.

Suddenly, Jasmona, Usha and other people around saw Dolly running ahead of the competitors with a consistent gap of more than 100 m.

The moment finally came when Dolly hit the bar, slowed down running and then limpingly fell down on the track.

Jasmona and Usha rushed towards her. Jasmona kept Dolly's head in her lap. Usha started sprinkling water over her face and tried to feed her water. Dolly was feeling exhausted with breathlessness and drowsiness. Soon the first aid team reached near them and started checkup and treatment.

Jasmona's eyes were searching for Rajat. She got annoyed at Rajat's absence in such a moment of lifetime achievement.

Rajat failed to make his presence in time because he could not run like the other participants accompanying him. He was managing to do a brisk walk and reached after everybody had settled there and Dolly had also recovered from the post-running exhaustion.

"Welcome, Mr Rajat! Welcome. The whole world is waiting for you." Seeing his clueless gestures, Jasmona said, "Still don't know what for? Hello, Mr Husband! Your wife won. She beat the previous record holders and has made a new record. For the first time ever a lady aged 50+ years has won in this category."

Just before Rajat could speak something, there was an announcement calling the winners near the stage. Dolly requested Jasmona to accompany her. Jasmona pulled Usha along, too. Rajat stayed back alone, with the crowd.

The pictures and videos of Dolly receiving the award from the hands of an iconic Olympic Gold Medal winner went viral within a few minutes.

Later on, while coming out of the venue, dozens of media channels surrounded Dolly for an interview. She was feeling suffocated. It was the first time in her life when she was the target of dozens of speaker-mikes.

She was finding it very difficult to handle hundreds of questions at a time. Rajat, badly mingled in the crowd, was struggling to get rid of the nuisance around and reach Dolly. Jasmona and Usha were trying their level best to manage the situation and control the mob of journalists and well-wishers.

One of those questions was "Whom do you give the credit for your win? Yourself or somebody else?"

"1% of the credit goes to me and the remaining 99% credit goes to Dr Dave, whom I lovingly call Jasmona Di," Dolly joyously yelled.

The flock then diverted towards Jasmona.

"Guys, let's meet in City Hospital, Andheri at 6 pm for your questions." Jasmona with a sparkling smile and soprano voice smartly diverted the storm.

That evening, the recreation hall of City Hospital was crowded like hell, more than the morning venue.

Jasmona was accompanied by Dolly, Rajat and Usha at the dais.

Rounds of multi-genre questions and prudent answers started and the session progressed very well. Meanwhile, a particular question caught the attention of everybody.

A TV News Channel Journalist asked, "Madam! A video went viral where Dolly Madam was struggling to recover from the fall and you could be heard shouting "Me No Pause, Me Play" repeatedly. I am asking this question, as I couldn't understand its meaning, and I think many people didn't understand it either. Can you please enlighten us?"

With a dose of laughter and ever shining bright smile, Jasmona started speaking in her sweet Mezzo-Soprano voice, "See, the so-called slogan, is primarily set of three words, extracted by breaking the spelling of MENOPAUSE.

I think everybody here is a social person, a family person and must be aware of menopause, either by default or by some fault. It's a natural transformational course in every woman's life. Every woman has to move into this phase of life after passing certain age, and it's not a big deal. It's a normal phenomenon, happening for ages in human societies.

But, historically it had been studied that one-in-hundred million cases of menopause are observed as the severest cases where the women had suffered death-like situations. A very few could survive and many succumbed.

Unfortunately, Dolly Madam was one of those one-in-hundred million severest cases of menopause. Dolly was suffering from this deadly phase, for the past one-and-half years. Because of those imbalances and disturbances in her mind & body, approximately one year ago, she met with an accident, where she suffered brain injury with multiple blood clots and half-body paralysis. She was admitted into the ICU at this hospital.

I, Dr Dave, came into the picture after her admission here. I studied her case in micro detail and started the treatment with a combination of conventional medical science and technology methods and innovative alternative treatment methods that I risked. The innovative methods are nothing but derived from basic human instincts and DNA blueprints of the sufferer and her near and dear ones.

After 12 months of treatment, the result is in front of you. The patient of the severest menopause case coupled with brain injury, paralysis and neurological disorders has won the half marathon race of 5 km category. Isn't it a miracle?"

The journalist responded, "Yes Mam! It's really a wonderful real-life story. But what is the meaning of that slogan?"

Jasmona laughed again to the fullest and then responded, "Ok, so, ME + NO + PAUSE. If you add these three words it becomes MENOPAUSE. I just broke a word into a meaningful set of small words without disturbing the original.

So, it's a moral boosting slogan for women. ME + NO + PAUSE means I will never pause in life in any situation. I will not stop in any adverse situations in life. I will never give up. I will never budge down.

Then there was ME + PLAY, which means, I will keep on playing in life. I will keep on living my life. I will keep on excelling in my life. I will keep on flying like birds.

The combination of these two is a worthy morale booster—I will not pause, I will play. I will never stop, I will keep on playing.

Though it may be labelled as an existing self-help quotation from self-help books, it is derived from a particular word, from a particular life situation of a woman. So, it's a woman-centric slogan."

Lots of applauds were received in reaction to Jasmona's wise answer.

The next day all the streams of media—print, electronic and digital were showering tons of praises to Dr Dave and appreciation for Dolly. The Chairman of City Hospital was very happy. City Hospital suddenly jumped the chart in a short period of one year after Jasmona's joining.

The next day, Jasmona got calls from Akshay and Anjali, who were praising her like Goddess who not only healed their mother but transformed her into a miraculous sports persona. They got all the information from social media and their mother.

Jasmona allowed them to come down to India to see their mother and stay for a few days with her. She declared a period of rest for Dolly for the coming month where she could run and play games if she found herself comfortable.

Anjali and Akshay came together with their families and stayed back for one month. They enjoyed the stories of their father who enacted as a singer, mimicry artist, mouth organ player and comedian. Surprisingly,

Rajat played the same characters in front of them too. Anjali and Akshay were so happy to see such a wonderful personality of their father, which they missed in their childhood. Jasmona kept on coming to join them for breakfast, lunch and dinner sessions.

One month passed. Anjali and Akshay returned back to their lives. Dolly's period of one month rest was also completed.

One late Saturday evening, Dolly called Jasmona, but Jasmona didn't pick up the call. Dolly got worried and was about to call her again but decided to wait for a few minutes.

There, the gem of doctor fraternity, multi-talented, multi-tasker, honest, warrior, risk-taker, brave, troubleshooter, hard worker, intelligent, modest, MD of City Hospital, who recently rose to heights of legendary name and overnight fame, owner of a gracefully beautiful face even at the age of 55, having looks 10 years younger than her biological age, known for evergreen brightest smiles, having sweet Mezzo-Soprano voice, charming speaking style, known for having golden heart known as delight as socialising, expert at the art of converting adversaries into benefits, despite all the visible positivities in her persona, she was a loner. A lonely person not by choice, but by destiny. Parents passed away a few years ago. No siblings as she was the only child. No near and dear ones, no genuine friends, not married. Top secret reasons, nobody knows. Such a nice person destined to be all alone inside four mute walls and deaf dumb roof.

She heard the ring tone. Through brimmed eyes, she saw it was Dolly. Amid sobbing whispers, she switched on the flight mode on her mobile and floated herself into clouds of chronicle insomnia.

Chapter 5

Pinnacle

The doorbell sound disturbed the deep sleep, rather annoyed Jasmona. She could hardly get any sleep early in the morning as the whole night was spent struggling for getting sleep.

"Oh! It's only 8 in the morning. Who the hell has come at this time on Sunday?" Murmuring irritatingly and yawning, Jasmona moved towards the main door.

Surprised with unexpected delight, Jasmona sighed when she saw Dolly at the door. "Dolly!" She giggled and hugged her. "What happened? Here, so early morning. Is anything wrong?"

Then she saw Rajat standing a few feet away in the lobby.

"Yes Di," Dolly whispered slightly nervous.

"What happened? Oh, first, come on inside." They all came inside, sat on the sofa and then Jasmona asked again, "Yes, tell me what happened? What brought you to me so early in the morning on Sunday?"

"Di! Earlier I was fortunate to see you every day. But for the past few days, I have started feeling so restless when I am not able to see you. It's hard to believe, but I feel that I am accustomed to you. Yesterday,

I thought you would be free, so I called up. But maybe you were busy, so you couldn't pick up the call. After some time when I tried again, I was told that the phone was out of coverage area. So, I got worried."

Rajat intervened, "Last night, she didn't sleep for a single minute. She kept on calling you and kept asking me to take her to your house. We didn't have your address, so we got it from the hospital in the morning."

Jasmona gave a grim look to Rajat and checked her mobile. She undid the flight mode and was surprised to see several missed calls from Dolly throughout the night. She got emotional and covered her face with folded hands. She talked to herself, *"Many people came into my life, but for the first time ever, somebody is so concerned about me, who didn't sleep the whole night because of me, kept on calling me because she was worried. Seems that she is serious, she is selfless, genuine with true love. Ok, let me talk to her."*

Jasmona uncovered her face, unfolded her hands and murmured with a light smile, "Why? Why were you worried so much about me? Why did you keep on calling me the whole night?"

Dolly got up from the chair, moved towards Jasmona and sat beside her feet. With brimmed eyes, she whispered, "Don't know, Di. I don't know. Since the moment you came into my life, I don't know why, but I find my twin soul in you, and I can't live without you. It's not that you did my treatment and healed me, that's why I am feeling some kind of obligation or emotional attachment towards you. But, since the very first moment that I saw you and heard you, I did fall in love with you. It's not that kind of love but soulful love between two human beings."

Jasmona wiped her tears, helped her up and whispered, "Let's move inside, in my bedroom. We will talk there.

"In the bedroom? But your family?" Dolly asked.

"I don't have any family. I am alone."

Dolly was surprised as she was unaware of that unusual fact. Actually, since the beginning, they had never ever spoken about Jasmona's personal life.

Rajat was also surprised and was about to speak, but Jasmona turned her head towards him and gave him a grim look.

Jasmona started moving towards her bedroom with Dolly. Rajat also followed them.

Jasmona bluntly stopped him. "Rajat! It's women's talk, so men are not allowed. You do one thing, leave Dolly here for a few hours and go back home. I will call you when Dolly would like to come back home. Ok?"

Rajat, with a confused face, gestured "as you ladies wish" and left from there.

After reaching into the bedroom, Jasmona asked Dolly to wait for some time as she would join her after she freshens up.

A few minutes later, they sat over the bed at farthest ends, facing each other, and the conversation continued.

"Di, it's shocking to me. Why didn't you marry?" emotional Dolly asked inquisitively.

"Oh, come on, Dolly, let bygones be bygones. No use talking about the past. I have already moulded myself as a destined loner." Jasmona tried to divert Dolly's emotional inquisitiveness about her personal life.

"What, Di? I am really feeling very bad to see the goddess of positivity suddenly talking negatively? If you really love me, please share your life story with me. Please don't let down my request. Maybe, I can help you out, maybe I can do something for you." Dolly's innocent naïve expressions couldn't melt hard frozen emotional icebergs deep down Jasmona's heart.

"Don't be emotional, Dolly, be practical. I am 55, I have learnt to live alone. Practically, the whole day is spent amid patients in the hospital. Only the night is the time when I am alone, and I spend that time talking to myself, talking to my reflection in the mirror. I have spent years and years like this, now I don't feel the need for anybody to fulfil my life. So, let's end the topic here and let's talk about something meaningful."

"No, Di. No. Please don't divert the topic. See, you heal everybody of their pains and help them have a better life. But you have hidden your own pain, untreated, and it's killing your own piece of mind."

Jasmona smiled slightly and murmured, "But that's my job. It's my duty to look after people and heal them."

"Correct. You are doing your duty towards people, towards the community. But, you are not doing your duty towards your own self. You are doing injustice to your own self. Still, there is time, age is just a number. You can still marry. You are so attractive even at this age that you will get tons of suitable proposals."

"Oh. No. No. No. It can't happen. Even if I want to marry, I can't marry," Jasmona responded in a painful voice with a choked throat.

"Why not, Di? Let me tell you, I was shocked to see you in the morning. The graceful and inspiring face, which I have been accustomed to watching, was so glum, gloomy and sullen."

"Ohhhh! That's the point! Dear, I had just gotten up after hearing the doorbell. I was in deep sleep. Actually, I don't get sleep at night, for many years, that's why." She realized that she had mistakenly spoken about her insomnia problem.

"What? You don't get sleep at night? How will you get sleep by being alone? Now, I caught you Di. Now, you have to listen to me." She got up and moved towards Jasmona and hugged her very tightly. She kept Jasmona's face into her loving warm lap and hushed like an inseparable twin soul, "Di, enough is enough. Stop punishing yourself. Please listen to me and get married."

Jasmona burst into tears and started sobbing like a destitute child. Dolly sensed the depth of emotional pain Jasmona was going through and kept on comforting her by massaging her back. Jasmona's cries blew Dolly's emotions, and she also started sobbing.

After some time, when the emotional outburst calmed down, Dolly wiped Jasmona's tears and cleaned her face with her dupatta. There were no words spoken. Keeping her head inclined, Jasmona was looking into nowhere, and Dolly was looking at her face.

A few more moments passed, Jasmona broke the silence and, again, amid tears, she sobbed. "Women never forget their first love. I also didn't forget. I remember each and every moment. But now, nothing can happen."

Dolly again took Jasmona's face in her lap.

Jasmona continued, "My love story started in my school, in Lucknow. It was like a childhood love story, which was known to only those two lovers and no one else. One was me, and the other was that naughty charming boy.

There were no reasons behind our love story, no starting point. It just happened, through eyes and anchored in our gullible hearts. We grew together, studied in the same class. We played together, danced together, sang together. He was very good at extracurricular activities. Like your Rajat, he was also very good at singing, dancing, comedy, jokes. He was a very good entertainer. He made me laugh.

I never saw him indulged in any kind of indecent behaviour or quarrelling with other children. But, sometimes, I heard about his darker sides. But as it never happened in front of me, I couldn't believe the half-baked news.

After 10+2, he joined B. Com, because his father was a Chartered Accountant and wanted his son to be the same. My parents were doctors and wanted me to be a doctor, so I joined medical college.

Even in college days, our secret love story continued. We still hadn't shared this with our parents.

Then after my MBBS and internship and before joining another college for post-graduation, marriage proposals started pouring in. I somehow was managing to distract my parent's attention by fabricating some or the other reasons. There, my boyfriend had completed his B. Com, M. Com and was on the verge of completing his CA.

One fine day, my parents told me about one high profile marriage proposal from the USA based NRI family of doctors, and, the highlight was that they were coming to see me in just two hours. The problem was that I had to attend the birthday party of a colleague. I managed to cancel the plan and stayed back at home.

I found myself in dilemma. I thought that I should tell my family about my love affair and should clear that I am not going to marry any man other than him. But then I did not want to upset my parents by telling them now. So I decided to reject the groom on some convincing grounds, and later on, considering suitable time and mood, I would tell my parents about my love interest and marriage plans.

Those moments came, the would-be groom's family reached our home and the formalities began as it happens generally. Things were going fine.

Suddenly, out of nowhere, my boyfriend reached there. I got shocked. Generally, I used to share everything with him, but that day, I couldn't talk to him because of so much hurry. I couldn't understand from where he got this information. And instead of calling me, he came there directly. For the first time ever, I saw the demonic side of him. He just started abusing, manhandling and fighting with my parents, the would-be groom and his parents. My family members knew him very well but never knew about our love affair.

Like a gully goon, he shouted and threatened everybody by declaring, "Jasmona is mine. Nobody can take Jasmona from me. Only and only I will marry Jasmona, nobody else can. If anything wrong happens, I will not spare anybody. I will kill everybody." He threw away the snacks, food and drinks, then ransacked the furniture and damaged the cars parked outside.

Everybody was shocked, I was frozen in panic. Somehow my parents managed to handle the grievances of that would-be groom's family and let them leave with unpleasant memories.

I ran to my room and locked it from inside. I didn't open the door despite my parent's several calls. I kept on crying the whole night. Whatever my boyfriend had done, was out of fear of losing me, and that, for once, could be considered to forgive him. But the way he abused and misbehaved with my parents broke my heart. I couldn't tolerate this. My own conscience was blaming me for all those mess-ups. The whole night, I spent thinking about what to do next? Suicidal tendencies were also scratching my head all night.

Meanwhile, my father registered an FIR against my boyfriend. Police arrested him and kept him in their custody for the whole night.

The next day, when I woke up, my mother asked me to get ready to go to the police station to submit the witness' statement. After completing the formalities, on my request, we submitted a case withdrawal application. He was released with a legal warning. I didn't make any eye contact with him or with his family members.

My father was not happy with my action of pardoning him. After returning home, my parents clearly told me that if still wanted to marry him, they would rather commit suicide.

I felt like a loser. I was completely broken.

I didn't respond to any of his calls or messages or his efforts for a patch-up.

I came to know that he was also invited to my colleague's birthday party through her brother. At that party, somebody told him about the marriage proposal. Anyhow, my love world had been destroyed forever for no fault of mine. The culprit was my own sweet boyfriend-turned-demonic-lover.

After that incident, hatred filled up inside me for Lucknow, for marriage, for love, for boyfriend. I decided to move to some other city for my PG. Fortunately, I had friends in Delhi who helped me a lot to stand up again on my own feet. I drowned myself in my profession.

Over the years, my parents brought several marriage proposals for me, but all their efforts went in vain. I couldn't imagine anybody else as my life partner, other than that person, and I had buried that demon forever in the graveyard of my memories.

So, since then, I am living my life in my profession only.

No place for any life partner in my life. The faces of my would-be life partner and ex-boyfriend are still alive in my eyes, nobody can replace them.

That's my story, dear Dolly."

Dolly, who was listening patiently, sighed and then asked, "What happened to your boyfriend? Where did he go? Where is he now and in what shape?

"My parents told me later that he got married and then had children. Actually, a few years ago, my parents died. So, I am getting no news from Lucknow."

"Di, Rajat is also from Lucknow. Can we ask him to find out your boyfriend?" Dolly surprised Jasmona.

"No. No. No. I am not interested in him anymore. And I am not interested in any husband stuff anymore. So, please leave me as I am, the way I am living my life. 5 years are left for retirement. Later on, I will work or not, I don't know,"

"Did you meet him ever after, or did you see him later?"

"Yes. Daily, I used to see him. His image is always there in my eyes, in my subconscious mind. After reaching home at night, it's his image only, it's his incomplete love only, which caused insomnia."

"That's ok, Di, but there should be some solution to your insomnia issue. Otherwise, it will be proved again that doctors are very bad patients. There must be some soulful thing to drive the aspirations of your life. Ok, having said that, I actually would like to know what aspirations you are carrying, which are still unfulfilled or you want to have after your retirement." Dolly was still trying to get some more information about Jasmona.

"Ooohhh! I remember the only unfulfilled aspiration I am carrying right now is that I want to have my own NGO for Women's Health Issues, like your case. I want to help those women who either can't have the awareness or are shy to share with anybody or can't afford such treatments, I want to provide them free-of-cost treatment for any kind of gynaec or other health issues, particularly in rural areas."

After listening to her aspirations, Dolly, with an open heart, said, "Ok, Di, now I want to say something. It's not because I want to do something under obligation to you or because you have given me this life. But I can say that it could be my vested interest, too. So, please don't turn down my idea.

Since my treatment is over now, there are no chances of seeing you on a daily basis. But, as I told you earlier, now I am badly accustomed to your presence, your touch, your face, your voice, rather I am badly obsessed with your existence. Honestly speaking, if I miss them, I fear, I could again fall into the nervous breakdown and all those scary symptoms.

Though Rajat has improved a lot and he can take care of me. But, Di, just consider yesterday night's case. I wanted to talk to you, and when it didn't happen, I couldn't sleep the whole night. I kept on calling you again and again like a lunatic. Why? Because I started feeling breathless. My mind and heart were filled with so many scary things. So, now you can understand how badly I need you.

So, it's my selfish wish. Please understand my emotions, I am not doing any emotional blackmailing, but the thoughts are coming from the bottom of my heart. Please leave this place and stay with us. We have twin-duplex bungalows in Juhu, earlier rented out, now lying vacant. I want to leave this bungalow and want to start a new life in a new place. Having you in my life, always visible, always near me, will keep on energising me to live further and inspiring me to do betterments in life.

"Oh, Dolly! You have brought me to the hardest dilemma of my life. How can a doctor accept an offer like that from a patient? I can even lose my job for accepting any such offer. Even if I ignore the official constraints, how could it be possible for me to become a liability upon you, by residing at your home without paying anything? It seems unethical, impractical and out of sheer emotional instincts." Jasmona opposed the idea.

Jasmona's response left Dolly uncomfortable for a moment. She thought something for a while and then said, "Ok, Di, if you feel such problems could arise, then please stay with us on paid rental basis. The same rent that you are paying here, pay us. Is that ok?"

"Oh, Dolly, means you have made up your mind that you will not leave me in any condition. By hook or by crook, you want me to be with you only."

"Yes, Di, if you want me to remain alive."

That Sunday Dolly and Jasmona kept on talking for many hours. Dolly turned down Rajat's intermittent calls by telling him that she would call him.

Late night, Jasmona, the iron lady, having a strong IQ and EQ, surrendered in front of the innocence of Dolly and agreed to stay with them.

Rajat was asked to come the next morning to bring Dolly back and escort Jasmona to the hospital.

The next morning, Rajat dropped Dolly home and then dropped Jasmona at the hospital.

They both were silent, while on the way to the hospital.

Suddenly, Jasmona whispered, "Yesterday, because of her adamant wish, I told Dolly my life story in detail."

"But not about our past, right?" Rajat asked curiously.

"I told her everything, except your name."

"Did she get any suspicions?"

"No! But she will get suspicious if you act foolish as you did then."

"No. No. No. I will not repeat the past mistakes, which spoiled my life forever."

"How was your life spoiled?"

"It's a spoiled life only where you are not in my life."

Jasmona couldn't tolerate Rajat's dishonest confession and slapped him.

Shocked by the slap, he slowed down the car and drove it sideways and stopped in the service lane. Rubbing his cheeks he asked, "What happened?"

"Whose life is spoiled Rajat? Yours or mine? You got married, had a lovely wife and had children... and me? I remained unmarried because of you, because of your idiocies. Bastard! You spoiled my life. Now, why are you halting here? Move, I am getting late." Jasmona vented out her frustrations and blasted at Rajat.

Being at the receiving end, no words entered his mind to respond. He decided it was better to drop Jasmona at the earliest.

After driving for a few minutes, the unwanted silence was irritating him. Some wise thoughts came to his mind out of creative curiosity, and he couldn't resist asking. "If you don't mind, can I ask a question?" Rajat broke the silence.

Jasmona didn't utter a single word.

"Is Dolly completely out of danger now?"

"Yes or No both. If you behave properly, then yes. If you don't behave properly, then no."

"One more question, if you don't mind. See, Dolly was just 49 years old when she faced menopause. Did you also face menopause, because you are 55 now?" Rajat felt like asking an intelligent question.

Rajat's absurd question provoked Jasmona beyond the grey shades of her balanced character. She couldn't control herself and again showered Rajat with slaps over his face.

Rajat again lost the balance over steering, slowed down the speed, drove the car sideways and parked in the service lane again.

Infuriated by Jasmona's action, Rajat asked with hollow confidence. "What happened this time? I asked a technical question."

"Bastard! Fool! Have you lost your mind? How dare you ask a woman such questions? No manners, no etiquettes, how to talk to a woman. Nowadays, sometimes I do feel, it happened for good that I couldn't marry you, else my life would also have been spoiled like poor Dolly's. You might have been a good lover, but not a good husband." Jasmona vented out the rest of her frustrations.

The slaps taught life lessons perfectly straight. Rajat understood that because of his oppressive deeds throughout his life, he has lost all the relations at home, and now, he would have to live with it or perish.

Out of curiosity once again he wished to ask something.

"No more questions, Rajat. simply drive the car, I am getting late."

Finally, after dropping Jasmona at the hospital, Rajat drove back home.

Dolly was eagerly waiting for him and told him the entire story of Jasmona. She also told him about her staying with them in their Juhu twin bungalows.

Rajat agreed to everything, as he didn't have any better choice.

Within a few days, the renovations had been done for the Juhu bungalows.

Those bungalows were fully-furnished high profile accommodations laced with modern-day amenities, bought by Rajat a few years back.

After some days, they shifted over there and started living happily.

Jasmona's management issued her a NOC for renting at a patient's place.

Dolly further improved a lot as Jasmona was always there for her. Jasmona's insomnia was also healing slowly as Dolly was there for emotional fulfilment.

Five years passed by without any unpleasant situations.

Dolly was now perfectly fit, better than she was in her younger days. She always used to praise Jasmona for her rejuvenation.

Rajat was nowadays known as Entertainer Uncle, as he used to make people laugh with his comic actions, jokes and melodious songs. Quite often he used to prepare food for Dolly and Jasmona. Some people asked him for trying his luck in Films, TV Serials, but he always used to turn down the hollow advice.

Akshay and Anjali were happily living life with their families in the USA and kept visiting their parents occasionally.

Jasmona was retired now and had started her NGO named **MNP-MP** (Me No Pause-Me Play) for helping women having health issues, particularly gynaec issues. Dolly started working for her as a helping hand. Jasmona didn't entertain any active help from Rajat.

Despite forced celibacy, Rajat was happy and led a healthy life at such an old age. But still hopeful that Dolly would oblige him with much-desired intimacy even at this age. Sometimes still fantasising about Jasmona.

More than anything, he was silently very happy from the bottom of his heart, for having Jasmona, his childhood love, in front of his eyes. Though he had regrets and guilt for spoiling her life, he used to keep on trying, from his end, to help her indirectly, which she could hardly be aware of. Though sometimes, when situations permitted, he used to try earning her goodwill, she never allowed Rajat to re-enter into her heart.

Rajat and Jasmona diligently maintained the secret of their past relationship.

All three senior citizens were excelling in their second innings, quite stress-free and fulfilling.

Whatever, be the mischievousness of destiny, all three souls together were happily mounted on the pinnacle of their life journey, which they never expected to be.

Glossary

Womanica	- Name of a company
ASAP	- As soon as possible
ICU	- Intensive Care Unit in a hospital
SOP	- System Operating Procedure
MD	- Managing Director
Kabhi sochta hu ki mein kuch kahu	- Hindi film song
Anulom Vilom, Bhastrika, Bhramari, Udgeet and Kapal Bhati.	- Yoga breathing exercises
Kanda Poha	- A veg breakfast dish
Pal bhar ke liye koi hame pyar kar le, jhootha hi sahi	- Hindi film song
Do din ke liye koi ekrar kar le, jootha hi sahi	
Hamne bahot tujhko chup chup ke dekha	

Dekh sakta hu mai kuch bhi hote hue,
nahi mai nahi dekh sakta tujhe rote hue - Hindi film song

Ae meri zoharaa zabi, tujhe maalum
nahi, tu abhi tak hai hasi aur mai javaan - Hindi film song

EQ   - Emotional Quotient

SQ   - Spirituality Quotient

PG   - Post Graduation

Dupatta   - Lady's cloth